pd

THE SECRET OF
THE KASHMIR SHAWL

TO NITA SMITH OF SAN FRANCISCO AND
ALL THE OTHER GIRLS WHO
ASKED FOR A CECY BOOK

CONTENTS

CONTENTS

THE SECRET OF THE KASHMIR SHAWL

CHAPTER I

THE SECRET BELL

ALL this fuss just to get a job. Cecy Duncan
tilted back the little beret that clung to her fair hair
and slumped down deeper into the bus seat. The
fuss had been mainly in getting her sister Carol and
their father to agree that she should take a job, any
job during vacation. Cecy had been in the West
with her Aunt Isabel, going to school there, and according to her own report, taking it easy while Carol
slaved at social service, caring for nursery children
and generally assisting their families.

"Well, we'll see what little Cecy can do to help
out," Cecy was confirming her resolutions. "Besides, this ad looks like something different, and
something different is exactly what I'm after."

Cecy Duncan, Carol's young sister, had had quite
a time of it when she and her chum Rosie Wells

spent one other vacation, ferreting out the story of the Wild Warning, one of the Melody Lane mysteries that had to do with that captivating little urchin, Polly Cobb, better known as Flinders. And her name wasn't even Polly Cobb, although she used to feel that should have been her name, since good kind Mrs. Cobb, Aunt Kate to Polly, had taken the child in with her own happy, though poor family of youngsters. This exciting experience was particularly vivid in Cecy's mind this morning.

"I wonder what has become of Flinders," she ruminated, recalling that the last the girls had heard of the interesting little Polly, was when she made the sensational recovery of a valuable and highly prized miniature of Nora Grant's baby. Nora Grant was a famous actress, and her baby had been threatened with kidnapping. This miniature was the one and only picture of the baby, little Sylvia, and its disappearance had caused the mother and other members of the actress' family great anxiety. When Flinders, Polly Cobb, recovered the picture Nora Grant promised to do great things for Flinders. That was the story of the Wild Warning.

"Strange she never attempted to get in touch with any of us," went on Cecy's thoughts, "and she seemed so spunky and high spirited. Well, I had better keep my mind on my own spunk, right now, if I'm going to get this job. I had no idea it was so far out and in so lonely a place."

Cecy was making her way along the road she had been directed to follow when she left the bus. Facing the facts now, Cecy realized it was quite different from merely talking it over with Carol and her father that morning, the night before, and on every occasion when she could get the chance, since she had come upon the ad in the little country paper. And that itself had been queer. Why should the country paper and not an important city paper have been selected? Carol declared sympathetically, that that made the matter suspicious. Mr. Duncan, the girls' father, himself a newspaper man, said positively:

"No little country paper like the Turnville Press could ever get an important ad, and it's sheer waste of time for you to bother with it, Cecy. But this is vacation time. Do as you please but keep close to shore."

"But, Dad, I've been to the agency and they vouch for this ad. And both you and Carol know the Newkirk Co-operative Agency is perfectly reliable, don't you?" Cecy had answered.

That had stopped them, as Cecy was now trying to re-assure herself. For when a reliable employment agency has investigated both the prospective employer as well as the one seeking employment, everything is supposed to be strictly as represented.

Cecy stopped and took the small printed slip out of her purse once more. She knew every word by heart but needed something real to fortify herself.

"Not that looking for a job is so serious, but a girl can run into dead-end streets just as well as a boy can these days. And little Cecy is just no good at jumping off dead-end streets. Too many movies, maybe. That dead-end street gang must have made an impression on me when I saw it out West with Aunt Isabel. Let's have another squint at this mysterious ad."

She smoothed out the clipping and leaned against a crooked old tree by the roadside as she read:

"Wanted. Young girl as companion to elderly lady. Must be cheerful, healthy and discreet. Only one sincerely interested in making good need apply." Then the directions were given, with the number of the bus to take and the way to reach Tanglewood, the name of the estate, probably.

"Why on earth should an elderly lady want a young girl as companion?" Cecy again deliberated. "And why must she be discreet?"

But the agency had assured Carol, who went to the office with Cecy, that the elderly lady had been fully investigated and was found to be reliable and respectable.

So there she was, Cecy Duncan, just home from school in the Midwest and going out after her first job.

It was a long walk from the bus line, and the bus line had been a long ride after the train ride. The day was quite warm now, and as she trudged along Cecy took off her blue sweater, smoothed down the sleeves of the new print dress and hoped she looked all right for the job of being a companion.

It couldn't be much farther; the bus man had told her to turn where all the letter boxes stood on their posts not far beyond a gas station. There were the boxes, she could see them now, and here came two girls; she would ask them the way to make sure.

"Hello!" they greeted her pleasantly as they came up to her. They were two girls about her own age, each with an arm twined around the other's waist and both smiling happily.

"I'm looking for a place called Tanglewood," Cecy said. "Is that it with the big white birches in front?"

"Yes, that's it," the girl with the dark hair answered.

"You are not, by any chance, answering that crazy ad, are you?" the other girl asked. She was fat and dimply and had reddish hair.

"Why—why, yes, I am," stammered Cecy. "Why?"

"Because the elderly lady," said the darker girl, "is Miss Benedict, and everyone knows *she* could never really want a young girl companion."

"Why? I mean, why not? I've come such a long way, all the way from—from—the city," Cecy said a little disconsolately.

"Oh, that's a shame," the other girl sympathized. "Mother saw that ad in the paper and she said she hoped no one would be taken in by it. I'm Janie Ward; we live over by the golf links. And this is Betty Fulton."

"Oh, yes," faltered Cecy, smiling at this sudden acquaintance. But she didn't say who she was. In fact, at that moment, she felt a little uncertain about who she might turn out to be, if she went any further into this silly business. Here were two very young girls, surely barely out of grammar school, and they were taking her to be just one of themselves. And she was Cecy Duncan almost ready for college!

She knew she looked "like a kid," as Carol had declared when she landed back from Aunt Isabel's, but she hadn't felt quite that young.

"Are you really going to Miss Benedict's?" asked Janie Ward, puzzled beyond concealment.

"Why, of course, I am. I want to work and I've always thought that queer elderly women have plenty of money. Surely this one must have or she wouldn't want to bring up a girl to be her companion," said Cecy, quite decidedly.

"Come on then, we'll walk back with you," offered Betty. "We're just taking a walk and we'll all toddle right along to Lady Benedict's," and she giggled happily.

They walked along the lovely country road three abreast, for there was plenty of room. Broad walks, broad streets and deeply set houses along the way, made Cecy think of dear old Melody Lane.

"There's the place," said Janie. "See the house away back there? You can hardly see it."

"Oh, yes," answered Cecy, looking back through the heavy trees that probably gave the place its name, Tanglewood. Somehow she couldn't seem very happy about the whole thing now. To be shut in way back there.

"Are you afraid of dogs?" Betty asked gently.

"Dogs? No I'm not afraid of well-behaved dogs. We used to have one," she replied wistfully.

"Well, Miss Benedict has dogs so don't try to go into the grounds. We know where the secret bell is that rings up at the house. It's just back of this big post."

"Secret bell!" The lump in Cecy's throat was hurting her now. She had not eaten much breakfast, she was in such a hurry to be on her way before Carol should think of something else to prevent her going at all.

"Are you ready?" whispered Janie. "Here goes!" and creeping in through the hedge to the other side of the big stone post that marked the entrance, Janie found and pulled the secret bell line.

"That rings the bell," Betty whispered to Cecy, "and in a minute someone will come to answer it."

"Who?" murmured Cecy. Somehow they were all whispering now.

"Can't tell. But we'll wait with you. Are you still sure you want to go in here and answer that ad?"

"Oh yes, yes of course. I intend to," declared Cecy, stoutly. But her thumping heart was trying to tell her a different story. Suppose she had not met the girls, she wouldn't even have been able to find that secret bell.

CHAPTER II

GETTING A JOB

THEY waited, and, of course, they were soon giggling. The girls told Cecy they could wait a while longer; it seemed they were going to town with Janie's mother who rode in Saturdays to do her heavy marketing.

Cecy was getting more and more nervous as they waited. There seemed to be something hidden in their manner, as if this Miss Benedict and her offered position were matters any girl should avoid running into.

"You know," Janie said, "people do a lot of talking about Miss Benedict, but mother says that's because she doesn't bother with them, just minds her own affairs."

"Here comes a man," said Cecy. "Who ever is he?"

"Oh, that's Pete," Betty told her. "He's all right. He works for Miss Benedict."

The man was coming along toward the big gate that was closed between the two stone entrance posts. It all seemed sort of jail-like to Cecy, for inside the hedge was a strong iron fence and the corner, where Janie had reached in to the bell pull, had just a small opening, up too high for a dog to break through.

Pete had a good smile, Cecy was thinking, and the way he pushed back his broken straw hat seemed friendly.

"I came about the ad," Cecy said through the bars. Janie and Betty had now turned to go, having first given Cecy a reassuring tug at her elbow.

"Oh, yes, yes. You're a girl—for the place?" Pete asked.

"I'd like to enquire about it," Cecy replied. She had her courage working hard now; she must not give in to silly ideas. She wanted work and this was the place to get it.

"You're pretty young. But then she said young, didn't she?" Peter was pulling the big iron latch of the gate up to release it. "Come along. And don't let her scare you. She's all right, Miss Benedict is."

"You mean not to be scared of the dog?"

"Oh, no," and Peter chuckled. "I mean Miss Benedict. Folks just don't understand her. But she's the best friend I ever had." He said that with such hearty sincerity that Cecy felt better instantly. Surely an old man like Pete ought to know.

Suddenly there came tearing down the path a

small black dog, barking as if his life depended upon
making a furious noise.

"Hey there, Snippy!" called out Pete. "Take it
easy." Then to Cecy, "Just goes on like that to
show off. He'll know you in a minute. Dogs are
like children. They want a lot of attention." He
was touching the little animal with the end of a light
stick he carried, touching him to give him "a lot of
attention."

"Here, Snippy," offered Cecy. "Hello, old fellow." Old fellow didn't seem to suit that sample of
dog, but she could think of nothing else to call the
tiny thing, a black-and-tan, the very sort of dog Cecy
had always been afraid of. There had been one in
old Margot's candy store, and not a child could ever
get past until Margot would call the dog off.

But the way Snippy sniffed along with them was
reassuring. He had completely stopped barking, in
fact he seemed glad of the company.

Anxious, very anxious to get this work, whatever
it might turn out to be, Cecy could not help feeling
a bit queer now that she was approaching it.
Ashamed of herself for such babyish nonsense, she
tried to think of what her chum, Rosie Wells,
might say and do if she were in her place. Cecy and
Rosie had always been the merriest of all the merry
girls, in their Melody Lane adventures, the telling
of which ran through the seven previous volumes of

this series. Lately, when Cecy came back East and Rosie stopped off for a "lark" on her way to the Catskill mountains, the girls had renewed their confidences. Both girls were more serious now but even more devoted to their girlhood comradeship. And now the thought of Rosie gave Cecy the required courage. After all, what could a job be but a job? Or was that a silly answer to a silly question?

Pete was talking, just saying things to be friendly. Snippy had dashed up to the door wanting to be first to announce the visitor.

"And don't mind the woman Malika, she's the cook," Pete whispered as the woman, Malika, appeared at the door.

She had a binder around her head and her skin was quite dark. That was all Cecy had time to notice just then.

"Here's the girl," said Pete crisply, and as Cecy was fixing up a smile, Malika said, "Come in, sit down. I'll tell Madam."

Her English showed training, Cecy was glad to notice. She might be Egyptian; Cecy remembered the young Egyptian woman who worked in the antique shop. She had the same queer deep dark eyes. But were Egyptians good cooks for American homes, she wondered?

The room she had been ushered into was not like any she had ever seen before. There were so many lamps standing up like silken trees all around and such a lot of red plush chairs. The curtains were of heavily embroidered velvet, and altogether Cecy got the feeling of being smothered in a drygoods factory. Too much of everything all over the place.

A voice sounded along the hall, then Miss Benedict entered the room.

"Good morning; you are early. That's a good sign. Sit over here where I can see you." Miss Benedict was short, stout and jolly looking, and she was wearing dark glasses. Her appearance brought a sense of relief to the anxious girl who had been thinking of a tall, erect severe looking woman, dispensing dour gloom.

"There; take the slipper chair. I like low chairs. My legs are so short."

Cecy hadn't said a word yet. She was just moving about and taking the chair pointed out to her. But she was no longer uncertain. This woman, Miss Benedict, must be good-natured; she looked it and she acted it. Of course, she did dress queerly, in those foreign robes. She was wearing a brilliant Japanese affair, but it was silk and looked simple enough to be washable.

"Now, tell me your name," demanded Miss Benedict quite sharply, thereby dropping the manner that had seemed jolly, and at once becoming very businesslike.

Cecy had learned from Carol, in her last minute advice when Carol found she could not go out to

Miss Benedict's with her sister, that one important point in seeking work was not to tell too much.

"Better just answer questions," Carol had pointed out. "Perhaps people like best to have their questions answered. Makes them feel more important."

So Cecy simply gave her name and then waited for the next question.

"I know you just came from the Middle West, that you have been there to school. That's very important. I wouldn't want a girl who has lived around here, that is in the rural districts—" Miss Benedict stopped suddenly tossed her head defiantly and shifted the dark glasses as if about to take them off. But she didn't.

Cecy's lips parted but she remembered Carol's advice. No need to say she used to live "around here in the rural districts." If Miss Benedict was satisfied that her stay in the West made her a westerner, why bring up Melody Lane? She didn't, and upon so small a matter much depended. Had Miss Benedict known that she was one of the girls whose school days, up to about now, had been spent in or about Melody Lane, Cecy would not have been hired for the job she so coveted.

"Of course, I have particulars from the agency," Miss Benedict went on, "but I like your manner. You know how to keep your mouth shut, don't you?"

"I know how to keep confidence, that is, I am sure I shall know my place," Cecy answered, having some

trouble in using phrases suitable for a person looking for a "situation."

"When I say can you keep your mouth shut I
know it doesn't sound very polite, but it's best to
make things clear. The girl I hire has to agree to
keep to herself what she may see or hear around
here. But don't worry that it will be anything
wrong," Miss Benedict seemed in a hurry to explain. "I'll promise you in turn that what I do is
my own business, or at least the business of those
who trust me. That's exactly it," she went on for
Cecy had not ventured a word, "I won't have others
interfere with me—as they'd like to," she added
shifting the dark glasses again but still not uncover-
ing her eyes.

"But what would my work be?" pressed Cecy.

"You would be a companion," Miss Benedict answered simply.

"Yes, I know. That's what the ad said," Cecy
pointed out. "But I don't know what that means."

"Well, it isn't hard work. I like a young girl because they make me feel younger myself, and a
young girl is—well, I just like young girls," she
added vaguely, and Cecy was trying to feel that it
was a good thing for her that she did.

"Yes, of course, Miss Benedict, I'll do all that I
can——"

"Do you write a fair hand?" the woman asked
next.

"They say I do——"

"That's important. I have a good bit of writing to do at times. I know from the agency that your folks are what we call genteel." She smiled at that. "Not that I believe one's manners are so important, but, well, you know lots of people do think so," she finished.

"I was afraid I would not seem just, well . . . ," and here Cecy stumbled into a laugh.

"That you would not appear to be in the servant's class? I know. Isn't that the silliest way for women and girls to advertise? 'Not the servant type,' they say. Well, anyone who is above her job would never suit me," declared Miss Benedict stoutly.

"But my real trouble is," declared Cecy determined this time to say something, "I have not yet been trained for any work."

"All the better. I'll train you myself. Besides, this isn't work in the ordinary sense of the word. When can you start in?"

"Why, any time. When would you want me?" asked Cecy, feeling more and more as if she were going to jail instead of going to work.

"Right away, say tomorrow? Yes, that's fine. Here's a few dollars," she was feeling in the long pocket of her loose robe, "take this then I'll know you will be sure to come back."

CHAPTER III

A DEAD LITTLE MOUSE

WHEN Miss Benedict pressed the money upon Cecy the girl felt she really should not take it. She had not earned anything yet, and maybe accepting money was not just the right thing to do. So she protested. Said she had her carfare and all that and didn't like to take money until she had at least begun to work.

"Tut, tut. Don't be proud, not that I don't like spirit. But you are just starting in and you may need a few dollars," Miss Benedict insisted, until Cecy gave in and put the money in her purse.

"Shall I wear—a uniform?" she asked timidly.

"Uniform!" Miss Benedict fairly hissed the word. "I should say not. Why should anyone wear a uniform except when it's most practical? Just fetch along your pretty school dresses. By the way, for a time at least, I would rather you did not go home very often. After a while it will be all right, but just at first it would probably be better to, well, sort of stay in," said the woman, who was now so plainly watching the door that opened on a porch off this room that she seemed too distracted to keep her mind on Cecy, and the work she was offering her. Cecy had heard a slight noise outside the door but thought it might be the little dog, Snippy, if she had bothered thinking of it at all.

But now Miss Benedict quickly removed the dark glasses from her eyes, put her finger to her lips to indicate silence for Cecy, and noiselessly stepped to the door. With one twist of the knob she swiftly opened it and the Egyptian woman, Malika, stumbled clumsily into the room.

"So, you were crouched there listening—" Miss Benedict began.

"No madam, I was not crouched there listening, as you charge me. See here, here it is," and she got to her knees, opening her hand. "Here—a little mouse!"

"Well," stammered Miss Benedict, "what of it? What about the little mouse?"

"Did you want Snippy to get it?"

"Oh, no, certainly not. A mouse, any mouse may have been poisoned. They're always after traps baited with poisoned cheese——"

"That is why, Miss Benedict, I crept into the door. I saw the mouse come in on the porch, and you see, I have got it."

"Yes, yes of course, Malika, that was wise, a good thing to keep the little mouse away from little Snippy," Miss Benedict now admitted.

"I knew you would think so. But—" The dark

woman was now standing and as Cecy watched her,
spellbound at the bit of drama, she saw her draw her
hand across her forehead, in a queer signlike symbol.
"But," the woman repeated, very deliberately, "you
have taken off your glasses!"

"Yes, yes so I did," flustered Miss Benedict.
"I'll put them right on again." But Cecy had a
good chance to notice what really lovely brown
eyes Miss Benedict had, before she again had them
behind the queerly shaped dark glasses. And she
wondered why she did that.

"I'll go now, Miss Benedict," Cecy managed to
say.

"Oh, wait just a minute. Malika, be sure you do
something, something definite about that little
mouse. Better get Peter to bury it. And bury it
some place where Snippy won't find it," ordered
Miss Benedict.

But as the woman turned away Cecy felt sure she
had discovered a menacing look in the dark rolling
eyes of the Egyptian woman, Malika.

That was queer. Could the foreign woman really
have been after the mouse? Or had she carried the
mouse with her for just the trap she had found herself caught in, when Miss Benedict came upon her
so suddenly?

"Plenty to find out there," Cecy was thinking as
she hurried back home to tell Carol and her father
that she really had the job.

Carol was just in from the Sunshine Day Nursery, which had been opened again and was flourishing under the guidance of a reorganized board of managers and also of a young woman's auxiliary. To achieve this success Carol and her friend, Cynthia Van Note, had worked all through a mystery and all its consequences, making the story "Stingyman's Alley," a true record of two girls, brave and victorious.

"But, Cecy," Carol was arguing, as Cecy knew very well she would, "how can you take a position without knowing more about it than——Well, after all, you just went there and this woman told you to come back——"

"And gave me five dollars to bind the bargain," Cecy was even now getting out the bag her Aunt Isabel had given her just before she came home.

"That's another thing." Carol seemed determined to find flaws in Cecy's arrangements. "Why should a strange woman have given you five dollars when she didn't owe you anything?"

"Just fell in love with me," Cecy chanted gaily. "Lots of people do, darling. And now please, sister, don't go turning this down to Dad. I think it's swell. A job and a mystery to work out. Like getting paid for dreaming." Cecy gave the new bag a rather violent slam down on the sofa. It just wouldn't stay open long enough to take in her things. "Let me see. Omit toothbrush if necessary" Rosie always says, "but never the sweet smells. Where's that one ounce of Nightmare the same Rosie gave me? What a name for good perfume," and she very carefully wrapped a very small but very pretty bottle in two spic-span hankies.

"I don't believe you should begin packing, Cecy," again her sister protested, "until we tell Dad."

"Carol Duncan, I'm going out there and I'm going to earn something like one hundred bucks this very vacation," Cecy proclaimed loudly. "If you're so particular you can come out with me yourself and look things over," she consented, dancing a few steps for punctuation.

"When? After you're there and have agreed to it all?"

"Oh, wait a minute. Whoa up there. You better not either. Don't come soon. Miss Benedict said—" She paused. If she told Carol Miss Benedict said she would prefer that Cecy had no callers soon, nor that she should go home soon, wouldn't that make Carol more suspicious?

"Why don't you want me to go? Any real reason, Cecy? Now, please be serious. We have done a lot of things in our young lives that perhaps we took chances in doing." Carol was referring evidently to such adventures as had made the plots for the other stories of this Melody Lane Series, "but we are older now and we should have more sense," she insisted.

"We have. Look at me. An honest young working woman with an airplane bag packed to the gills, five strange dollars in my purse—Oh, Sis, be a sport. Have confidence in my judgment. I know Miss Benedict is just what she seems to be. Besides, haven't you the personal word of that first class agency that they know her? All about her?"

"Well, I suppose so," said Carol very slowly, her voice dropping its tone of protest. "But, Cecy dear, you are my little sister and we really are not driven to the point of sending you out to work during your vacation, you know."

"Oh, no? Who goes out to work all year 'round now and doesn't even have any vacation?"

Cecy had turned to her sister with an impulsive little caress and for a moment the two girls clung to each other. Yes, Cecy was growing up. In fact, she had grown up a lot in the time spent West with their Aunt Isabel. And, after all, Carol was trying to convince herself, what is so strange about a good healthy girl wanting to work during vacation?

"Of course, darling," she said, as Cecy again flew to the closet for something else to go into that bag, "it is not the point of your going to work, that I'm worrying about; it's the sort of work it may be."

"You mean the sort of work we don't know it is? Well, that is a little unusual, I'll admit. But it pays, it pays already, and we can't even guess whether I'm to wash dishes, bathe and trot out Snippy or write personal letters, like any swell social secretary. That's what makes it so fascinating."

Which was not the best argument to offer Carol. Here is exactly where Cecy should have practised that new system of hers, and not said so much. It took more time and strategy to fix up the new suspicions than it did to cool Carol down in the first place. And if Carol had ever guessed what Cecy thought of that dark sinister creature, Malika, nothing could have patched things up.

"And I hope Ken is coming to take us to the movies tonight," Cecy tactfully changed the subject. "I'd love a nice long movie with a couple of—well, maybe a couple of good horse races and a murder or two. I like them noisy," laughed Cecy, while Carol shook her head in complete bewilderment.

Ken Powell, Carol's young friend, did come and he took them to the movies that evening. Because he was a young lawyer and said to be a smart one, too, Cecy was careful not to get into any discussion about Miss Benedict's unknown work. He might be too good at guessing, or he might even know this queer Miss Benedict. Feeling none too sure that she would actually get off to that already famous job the next morning, Cecy outdid herself in being jolly, as she said to Carol, "the life of every party which included nice young men like Ken Powell."

Ken was nice too, and he watched Cecy even at the risk of appearing silly to Carol, as Cecy led all conversation both before and after the movie, with accounts of the "wild times" she and her young friends had had at the Western School.

"I never could see any fun in such pranks," Carol commented once. "What's so smart about playing tricks on others when *you* know all about it and *they* know nothing about it?"

"But it's lots of fun, just the same," her sister insisted. "You should have seen Splutter Hays slide down the study hall stairs on that banana skin." And the memory of that childish prank just set Cecy laughing about it as fresh as new paint.

"Too silly to talk about," murmured the disgusted Carol.

"Oh, Sis, don't be a prissy," taunted Cecy. "I'll bet you played lots of pranks at high school a lot sillier than that."

"I'll bet she did too," chimed in Ken. "In fact she told me she did."

"Here, here! You two!" Carol checked their mirth "I'll admit it's all very, very funny. But here's the place we get our hot chocolate and it makes little girls and boys sleep just like tops, after the movies."

CHAPTER IV

THE CONSPIRATOR

THAT was the night before, and this was the
next day. And now Cecy was actually out there at
Miss Benedicts. She had been shown to her room
by the scowling Malika, and Miss Benedict was busy
with some man down stairs in the overstuffed living-
room. Cecy could hear their voices.

Malika seemed to be hanging around; she did not
turn to leave Cecy although Cecy plainly wanted to
close the door. But not in her face; even the scowling maid, whom Cecy was secretly calling Sourpuss,
might not like a door closed in her very face.

"All right, Malika; I guess I'll find everything,"
Cecy said by way of tactful dismissal.

"Oh, yes, I guess you will." She actually stepped
inside the door now. "You think you're going to
work here?" she didn't ask but sort of sneered.

"Think so? I know I am. Why?" Cecy wasn't
going to give in to any threats, even implied threats.

"Don't be too sure." The foreign woman was
wearing an old sweater and she now thrust both her
hands deep into the pockets until they bulged the

25

sweater out like some lumber-jack's coat. "Other girls come here too, but they don't stay long."

"Oh, but I like it here. I'm sure to stay. Miss Benedict and I are great friends."

"You know Miss Benedict?" she asked that in a very different voice, showing surprise and sudden interest.

"Why yes, of course I do," replied Cecy honestly enough. She did know Miss Benedict, didn't she?

"That's fine." The brazen woman deliberately sat down on the pretty chintz chair. "Then maybe you and I get along all right. We work together, eh?"

"Work together?" Cecy was thinking fast. She must be very wise now if ever. "Why, of course," she spoke up. "You know the place and I don't. You can tell me what I need to do, can't you, Malika?"

The woman got up and crossed the room to where Cecy stood with her back to the dresser. As she approached her Cecy was more sure than ever that this was an evil person, her very touch, as she laid her grimy dark hand on Cecy's to compel closer confidence, made the young girl shudder. But she must not let the woman see she suspected her. So she was smiling, listening, friendly.

"She's queer, you know," Malika referred to Miss Benedict, "and you have to watch out."

"Watch out? What for?"

"She know how to make trouble, plenty. I came here me, Malika Adabi all the way from my own country, because I must find this woman. I have found her." This last she said as if intoning a dire, ominous threat.

The menacing manner meant more than the woman's words. She was saying she had come from afar to find Miss Benedict and she had found her. Well, what of it? Cecy wondered. She didn't seem to be doing anything about it.

"If I could trust you——"

"Not to do anything against Miss Benedict, Malika," Cecy interrupted. "We might as well understand that right now."

"Against her. Who said anything against her? She's a foolish old woman and she doesn't know her danger, that's all. Well, I heard her ask you if you could keep your mouth shut. *This* is one of the times," and she turned suddenly, leaving the room on those soundless slippers, and closing the door silently behind her.

"Well," Cecy sighed speculatively, "and what might all that mean? I never did like these foreign beauties," she was reminding herself. "We had one, a dead ringer for this lady in our old Splatter Castle. I forget what her name was." She was thinking back to the story of the Forbidden Trail. Yes, there had been one of the queer dark women in that mystery, too.

"But she needn't think she can scare me off," the girl was deciding. "I'm going to get paid for *this* vacation if I have to fight a whole Foreign Legion to do it," and she put her green sweater in the bottom drawer of the honey maple chest, with the pretty medallion glass hanging over its top.

She had not had any conversation, since she came, with Miss Benedict. The strange man whom she had glimpsed, was evidently still talking with her down in the living room. Should she go down stairs and busy herself at something?

"Maybe I can give Snippy a run," she concluded, for it was embarrassing to be waiting around and not know where to go or what to do.

At the top of the stairs she stopped; there were voices at the front door. Miss Benedict was letting her caller out.

"You had better think it over," the man's oily voice murmured.

"I resent your implications," Miss Benedict said haughtily, "and I have nothing to think over. You must not come here again."

"Unless—I have to. I merely take orders and always carry them out. Always, Madam Benedict, Arama, carries out his orders."

There was plainly a threat in the way the man said that. Cecy, undecided whether to turn back to her room or to go down stairs to Miss Benedict, just stood there. She heard Miss Benedict murmur:

"Dear me! What a nuisance." And she saw her put her hand to her breast as if her heart had been beating too quickly. Then she turned and saw Cecy.

"Oh, there you are," she called cheerily. "Come right along down. I've been so busy I haven't even seen you."

Miss Benedict had gone into the small room off the hall; it was like a bay window against the porch. Cecy followed her in and took the chair pointed out to her.

Miss Benedict was plainly excited. Her round face was flushed and she was recklessly dangling in her hand those queer shaped dark glasses. They seemed to be shaped with sides, like boxes without covers.

"My dear! I'm so glad you're here. I never needed some one with me more than I do this very day," and the woman sank back as if exhausted. "Those awful people! Be sure that door is closed tight." She said this last almost in a whisper, and Cecy knew she wanted the door closed against the sneaking Malika.

Now Cecy could see, or she thought she could, what her work was to be. Miss Benedict, in some mysterious way seemed to be at the mercy of Malika, and that strange man who had the same foreign accent.

"Let me get you a glass of water, Miss Benedict," she began.

"Oh, no. Not just now. I don't want Malika to guess that I'm upset. I have to hold my own——" But her face showed more stress than Cecy believed good for her.

"Don't you worry about Malika," Cecy spoke bravely. "I'm not afraid of her nor of her kind either. I'll just go right out and bring you in a drink. I could make you a cup of tea in a jiffy," she offered. "We girls are just the best jiffy tea makers you ever saw."

"You're going to be a treasure," murmured the woman who was now subsiding into her normal mannerisms. "When I want a cup of tea I have to give time enough for the cooking of——"

"I know. Your tea-atite cools off before you get it," said Cecy, going out at once to the kitchen.

"Tea-atite," repeated Miss Benedict. "Oh, I see. Like appetite. She's a smart girl, and exactly what I need. Perhaps with her I'll be able to get clear of the scamps." She was fanning vigorously now.

When Cecy returned with the tea tray she brought along a beautiful early rose she had found by the kitchen sink. She had it standing in a neat little empty olive bottle.

"I didn't want to ask Malika for a vase, but perhaps she intended to bring it in to you herself," Cecy explained.

"No, indeed. No roses for me these days. It

seems Malika is bent on—well, maybe she intends to wear me down by her bad manners." She was sipping the fragrant tea and eating a cookie. "You certainly are a jiffy tea-maker," complimented Miss Benedict. "And I was right in insisting upon a young girl. The older 'girls' would wait to test the tea themselves first."

This sparkle of humor was already endearing the woman to Cecy. Entirely ignorant of what could be the secret of these foreigners' influence upon her, Cecy easily guessed they must be wrong, and Miss Benedict right. And people called her queer. Even the two girls, Janie and Betty had told her that, the day she had come to see about the job.

But Cecy could feel a tense uneasiness about the place; even out in the kitchen. Malika, who usually sneaked around was hollering at Peter to "fetch in the vegetables and be quick about it," while she just missed stepping on Snippy's paw and made him yelp anyhow.

It was morbid, this place with no other girls or young people around. Cecy had always had girls with her, and while she tried to help Miss Benedict over her anxiety without knowing what was causing it, her resolution to stay here and earn that good money was weakening.

"You were with an aunt in the Midwest? Did you say in Cleveland?" Miss Benedict asked suddenly.

"Not in Cleveland, in a town called Watchton outside or rather this side of Elgin, Illinois," Cecy answered.

"Oh, yes. Elgin is the great watch making place, I remember. And you helped your aunt?"

"Well, I went to school. That was why I went to Aunt Isabel's." Cecy remembered Miss Benedict had said she did not want to employ anyone from around Rumson. She said, very emphatically, she preferred some stranger to anyone from that part of the country. So Cecy quickly checked herself in explaining any more about going to her Aunt Isabel's. "But I did little things for Aunt Isabel, of course," she continued, "and she always said she liked my tea."

"Are you sure that side window on the porch is closed?" Miss Benedict began again in that anxious, secretive way.

Cecy got up and touched the bolt that held the double glass casement window together. It was closed. But she saw the little dog sniffing around on that end of the porch and she knew Malika was not far away.

CHAPTER V

THE UNEXPECTED

It must have been the training with her Aunt
Isabel. At any rate, Cecy knew she must not disturb
Miss Benedict by letting her know anything of her
suspicions about the housemaid. She would earn
her money; that she had promised herself to do, and
she was earning it now in protecting the woman who
had so strangely employed her.

Cecy left the window and smiled at Miss Benedict.

"I hope you are going to trust me," she said indifferently. "After all, maybe I'm just as smart as
—the rest of them."

"You are. I know you are. And they'll never
even suspect it. How wonderful to think you came
to me," Miss Benedict said in an undertone.

"Wouldn't you like to go out for a little walk
this lovely morning?" Cecy asked Miss Benedict.
She felt she would "blow up" if she had to sit there
in that tense atmosphere and not even have a little
exercise to keep her from fidgeting. Besides, she
wanted to get away from Malika.

"We could, couldn't we? Yes, the very thing. Then I can show you around. I have really quite a nice place here, don't you think so?"

It was far out from the house, under a big elm tree that they finally stopped to rest. The bench had a leather cushion which Miss Benedict explained had belonged to an old auto. Peter, it seemed, liked to sit under the elm, far enough away from the house to insure a respite from the sulky Malika's insistent orders.

"You are too smart a girl not to be wondering about this," Miss Benedict began frankly. "But I have to ask you to be patient. Just put up with it for a short time, then I'll promise you will have company and you won't be lonely."

"Oh, I've only just come; I'm not lonely. You are a lot like Aunt Isabel," Cecy assured the kindly woman, "and I'm very glad to work for you. My sister, Carol, has much harder work in a day nursery for poor children," she ventured. "I'm sure no one could call sitting around like this, in these lovely grounds, work at all." She glanced around at the beautiful trees, saw the strong early summer sun cutting through them to dapple the grass into grotesque figures. And she noticed that one ray of the glancing light seemed to rest upon Miss Benedict's soft, iron gray hair.

"Tonight you may phone your sister, if you care to. They may be anxious about letting so young a girl come way out here," Miss Benedict said next. "I realize that."

"Oh, thank you. I would like to," Cecy agreed eagerly. "But please don't worry about me, Miss Benedict, I'm perfectly all right, except that I would like to be doing something useful."

"You are, indeed you are. Anyone can dash around with a broom or a duster and make a racket, but it takes a special someone to do just what I need to have done now." This was a very serious statement.

"Of course I'm perfectly satisfied——"

"But very much perplexed." Miss Benedict again put on those hideous glasses. "You see, my dear, I have been travelling and when I went into the desert, far outside of Cairo, Egypt, I ran into some—well, let's call them thieves. Once people of this kind get their claws into a foolish tourist they dig deeper and deeper. And their superstitions, which can be so fascinating at first," she paused, then continued, "are like a web that weaves menacing bonds around unsuspecting strangers. You have heard of the occultism of the East?" Cecy nodded. "That's one thing they twist to their advantage— one of a great many tricks they employ."

"And Malika is from the Far East?"

"Yes, she is. She followed me here." Miss Benedict had lowered her voice although Cecy felt there was no one near. "And I'm keeping her on.

It's the easiest way, for a little while. Don't worry. She carries no knives under those loose fitting clothes, nor can these slick agents she sends here, scare me into any of their deals. You and I are smart enough to get out of their clutches," and Miss Benedict rose resolutely, her head high and her arm firm upon Cecy's.

The possible mysterious meaning of all Miss Benedict's remarks were beginning to excite Cecy. The foreign woman, with her sneaky ways, was bad enough, but now there was also a foreign man in the plot. The one who had been talking to Miss Benedict when Cecy came, certainly was the very one Miss Benedict referred to as one of "the slick agents" Malika was trying to trick her with. But about what? Why should these Egyptians have followed Miss Benedict all the way from Cairo to America? As if sensing Cecy's secret questions, Miss Benedict said:

"We hear a lot about gangsters in this country, and how once they get an unfortunate in their clutches there is no escape. Well, that idea did not originate in America. The fear of that sort of sinister power has always been used all over the world. Wicked people have built it up through superstitions, and still work with that same fear among the superstitious. Well, I'm not afraid, nor am I superstitious. But we have to be smart and pretty tricky to fool them. Then, when we are ready, we can turn upon them and watch them run. Listen!" she pulled Cecy's arm to hold her back. "There is some one over in that clump of elderberry bushes. Here, let's sit down again. Here's a bench."

"Oh, it's Snippy," Cecy exclaimed, as the little black dog dashed out of the bushes and sprang into its mistress' lap. He was wild with joy. He sniffed and threw his ears back then jumped up straight, his ears and his small body seemingly ready to spring at some hidden foe. He even barked a warning and Miss Benedict gave Cecy a knowing look.

"He's been frightened," she whispered, "and now he's daring someone to come get him."

"I'll run over and look in the bushes——"

"No, let them get away. We are not ready yet to defy them. We must wait until we are sure they can't fight back."

"Oh, of course, Miss Benedict," Cecy subsided, although she could see no sense in the argument.

Soothing the nervous little dog provided a distraction. Cecy remarked that maybe he had only seen a squirrel, and Miss Benedict smiled indulgently at that idea. Then she asked Cecy about what Malika had said to her when she came.

"She was rude, of course, but I was prepared for that," Cecy answered. "She asked if I knew you and was much surprised when I said I did. I do, don't I, Miss Benedict?"

"Certainly you do. And I'm glad you were smart enough for her. I knew you would be. But that gives me an idea. Suppose you call me Aunt Bessie. My name is Elizabeth but they call me Bessie," she explained. "If that old termagant Malika believes I have relatives around here she might not be so sure of herself. How about it?"

"Why, certainly," Cecy readily agreed. "It would make it more pleasant for me, too. Just having left Aunt Isabel it comes natural to say aunt to you."

"She'd likely be jealous, your Aunt Isabel. Well, your aunt and I must get acquainted some time. Both sharing the company of a fine young girl like you, we have a lot in common." She patted Cecy's hand at that. "So Malika wanted you to work with her, did she? She didn't waste much time about it, did she?"

"Perhaps I should have pretended to agree with her," Cecy said very slowly, showing she should not and could not have pretended anything of the kind.

"No, I don't think so. She wouldn't have believed you. Perhaps that was what she was trying you out for: to see if you would try to trick her. Oh, well!" Miss Benedict sighed. "Now that there are two of us I don't feel so trapped. There are times, dear, when an old lady like me can overdo her own courage. Just little prickly fears that warn me after all, I'm just Bessie Benedict, and these thieves have had a lot of experience in the game they play."

"But, don't you think, Aunt Bessie," she used the new name lovingly, "they just play on people? If we are careful, whatever their plans are, we ought to be able to get the better of them. As you say, they work with the fear of superstition, and we are not afraid nor superstitious." There was a defiant ring in that clear statement.

"I'd give three cheers only I don't want those bushes to hear me," declared Aunt Bessie. "And I feel rather mean not to tell you more about this business," she admitted. "But if I told you, your knowing it might spoil things. You might not always be able to act innocent, you know. And that's important just now."

"Please don't worry about me. I'm having a grand time. And, when I talk to the family this evening, I'm sure they'll be satisfied too," Cecy declared. "I did have a time convincing Dad and my sister Carol that this was the one best place for me," she admitted, "but when they hear me talk tonight, I know I can convince them that it really is."

A lovely long ride in a car which Peter drove that afternoon, dispelled much of the gloom that had surrounded Aunt Bessie's attempt to make some things clear to Cecy, while hiding the real story of her queer mixup with Malika and her confederates.

The lovely fresh early summer was forcing both green and flowers to their joyous beauty; the wonderful massive bushes of bloom, the lilacs, the rhododendrons, the early hydrangeas, and the long stretches of fence hidden completely under rambler roses—all affording the irresistible beauty that only the old country estates, free from cultivation's restrictions, ever attain.

"Oh, it's all so beautiful!" Cecy exhaled, barely forming the words.

"Yes, it is, isn't it?" agreed her companion. "You do love the country, don't you?"

"Well, yes, I suppose I do," faltered Cecy. "You see, we lived in a lonely country—" She checked herself just in time. She was about to say she had lived in Melody Lane, but remembered that Miss Benedict had said that she preferred someone who had not lived "around here."

Peter was just swinging his car into the curve that would lead them to the Tanglewood driveway.

"Yes," sighed Miss Benedict, "I love the country myself and hate to think of leaving it!"

"Leaving it, Aunt Bessie?"

"Yes, my dear. I had not meant to tell you yet, but we are going away, you and I, to live for a time in a city apartment."

"Oh, I hadn't thought of going away," Cecy exclaimed, disappointment in her voice.

"It won't be far and perhaps not for long, dear. But it's best for me to take this step. I will be helping a very dear young friend, and I will be getting away from that old Egyptian threat. I hope."

CHAPTER VI

BUSH WITH BLAZING EYES

CECY was completely surprised by Miss Benedict's announcement that she would soon leave the country place to help a young friend and to escape the threats of Malika and her confederates. Would her father and Carol consent to her going with Miss Benedict?

As they were ready to leave the auto, Miss Benedict had tried to reassure Cecy. It was impossible for her not to notice the girl's anxiety.

"There are lovely places near New York in New Jersey and not far from here," she explained. "And going there would really bring you nearer to your own home, wouldn't it?" she asked, kindly.

"Oh, yes, in Northern New Jersey, just outside of Newkirk there are plenty of lovely places and transportation through that district is splendid," Cecy replied.

"Yes, yes, my dear. Well, don't worry. Your Aunt Bessie will take good care of you," the woman finished, and Cecy knew that she would.

But on the telephone that evening, talking ex-

citedly to Carol in their first conversation since she
had left home, Cecy found herself floundering sadly
in her attempts to assure her sister that everything
was simply fine.   This sort of chatter sounded rather
silly when Cecy was trying to talk about her new
job, but wasn't the job very silly in itself?   She re-
ported that she had been out riding, and that the
country in Northern New Jersey was simply beautiful in this early summer; that she had been acting as
a real companion to Miss Benedict whom she was
now calling Aunt Bessie, and that she was going to
take a bus ride home in a few days.   Somehow it all
sounded very unimportant, and her sister, experienced and wiser in business affairs than was Cecy,
gave the impression that that was exactly what she
thought about the whole thing.

"But listen, Sis," Cecy whispered into the telephone receiver, "there's a lot more: things I can't
say over the wire, you know."

"Why, Cecy," came back Carol's voice, "why
should there be a lot of things you can't say over
the wire?   That just makes it worse."

"Oh, Carol," pleaded Cecy "please don't be too
exacting——"

"I see.   I understand.   You are not free just now.
Just say yes or no."

"That's it," Cecy answered.

"I understand, dear.   Sorry I sounded like an old
bear," Carol gave a reassuring little laugh with that.

"And you don't know how proud Dad is. Keeps blowing about his two girls in business. I tell you, Kid, I guess you had the right idea after all. No girl is educated today who couldn't earn her living in a pinch."

"That's what *I* think," sang back Cecy. "Of course I miss you and Dad and Rosie." She paused to swallow a choke. "But if it was all fun it wouldn't be working."

But finally she said enough and withheld enough to satisfy Carol that she would tell her a lot more when she went home in a few days, and reluctantly, very reluctantly the sisters finally said goodnight.

The telephone was in a little ell within Miss Benedict's bedroom, a very private corner and at the other side of the room from the hall. Malika could never listen there unless she were uncanny enough to hang on to the outside of the house. Leaving the little corner after talking with Carol, Cecy stopped to speak with Miss Benedict who was already in bed, all propped up beside her foreign looking bedside table, with its bejeweled lamp and its little golden god incense burner giving out a film of fragrant incense smoke.

"Sit down, dear, over here in the Turkish chair. I wonder why I ever gathered all this junk," Miss Benedict said, indicating the foreign pieces. "I must have been infatuated with the idea of antiquity. Carted them all the way from the Far East and I could pick up better on the East Side of New York."

"Oh, they're lovely," Cecy felt bound to say, examining the brass stool with its hammered figures and wondering what they represented.

"Truck. I hate them now and will throw them all out——" she paused, then added, "soon. Now listen, my dear. You can leave your door open between our rooms or close it, just as you wish, but don't be afraid. Snippy sleeps in his basket over there, and is up and flying around madly if a strange step so much as touches a porch, back or front."

Cecy smiled agreeably. She was a little more lonely since she had talked with Carol. This thing of being just one girl, instead of one of a crowd of girls, as Cecy and Carol and Rosie and Thalley had always been in their interesting young lives, was even at this early date becoming gloomy to Cecy. What wouldn't she give for one grand gab fest with her chum Rosie Wells right now?

But this was her job and Aunt Bessie was talking.

"Your bed and mine are in opposite sides of the rooms," she was saying, "so our lights will not flash at us, if you want your door open between."

"Yes, I do, Aunt Bessie. Aunt Isabel's room and mine were connecting."

"Bless that dear Aunt Isabel," said Miss Benedict, "she seems to have prepared the way for me."

Cecy laughed, a real gurgling little laugh. "Can I get you anything before I settle down?" she asked.

"Not a thing—oh, yes. Suppose you go out and collect Snippy. Malika holds him back until I ring for him. She is cultivating the love of that dog for her own sake, not for his."

So Cecy went down stairs to find the little dog. It was not yet completely dark, just a lovely young summer evening, soft with Spring's magic touch still lingering, and rich with the fragrance of Summer's effulgence bursting forth. As she raced down the stairs and through the house to the different doors calling and whistling for Snippy, Cecy was caught with the dread she had been desperately trying to conquer. The place was too solitary, with just herself and Miss Benedict, and that menacing woman, Malika, sneaking about. It would be so much better if Peter, the chauffeur lived in. Why didn't he, she wondered.

"Here Snippy! Snippy! Snippy!"

Her voice rang out clear from the back door now, and in answer she heard a timid yelp, an answer from Snippy. But he was not running to her. She waited, listened, then called again. But there was no answer this time.

"I'll have to go get him."

Down the long narrow path that led to the gardens, she skipped along, calling, whistling, and listening.

"I certainly heard him. Oh, there's a rustle in the

syringa bushes," she decided. "He must be over there."

Not pausing to let her courage wane, she kept on down the path to the great clump of tangled bushes near the end.

"Snippy, Snippy!" she called. "Come here. Where are you?"

At a stir around the drooping syringa bush Cecy ducked to look under.

"Oh!" she screamed, in a wild shriek.

She was staring at an object behind the bush, something with two blazing eyes, at least they were two round holes of light that looked like eyes, surrounded by something red. Too frightened to move at first, she saw that the thing itself didn't move, that its height was about that which a person would stand to, and then, all at once Snippy dashed out to her.

"Oh, Snippy!" she murmured, catching up the little animal and dashing back over the now darkened path. "Snippy, Snippy!" she whispered to the little creature that burrowed under her arm. "What was it? What held you there? If only you could tell me."

Within the house she hurried to Miss Benedict's room. Determined to hold no secrets from her friend and employer, breathlessly she told of the blazing eyes in the bush.

"How awful!" exclaimed the woman, getting out of bed and slipping into her robe. "We must find out at once——"

"Wait, Aunt Bessie," Cecy stopped her. "Don't let's do anything until we talk about this. That's just a trick of some kind. The kind of trick people like Malika think they can scare girls like me with. But they can't," she declared stoutly.

"Child!" exclaimed the woman in surprise. "How wise you are."

"Oh, no, not so very wise. But you see, Aunt Bessie, my sister and a lot of our girl friends have been doing things like that, and people exactly like Malika have objected to them, so we have often been scared before. But we are wiser now and we don't scare so easily."

"You mean Malika is trying to scare you away? To get you to give up being here with me? I don't understand, dear."

"I don't either, completely," admitted Cecy. "But I know that there is no natural burning bush unless it's in a bonfire. And that thing had blazing eyes."

"Oh, I'm frightened for you when I even think of it."

"Don't be, Aunt Bessie. It just makes it all the more interesting. Let's pretend we are scared to death. Then perhaps she won't try anything worse."

In spite of her bravado, Cecy's voice shook a
little. She put the grateful Snippy gently into his
basket, then filled his saucer with water from the
faucet. She was more angry than scared. As if a
girl her age was to be scared by some silly trick.

But it was what the whole thing might mean that
really mattered. No woman, not even a woman
like Malika would concoct a trick like that without
good reason. But what was the reason?

Poor little Snippy lapped up the cool water, while
Miss Benedict slipped out of her robe and agreed
with Cecy that the best thing to do would be to pretend the trick had worked. There was not a doubt
in Cecy's mind that it had been a trick and that
Malika was at the bottom of it.

CHAPTER VII

A HURRIED TRIP

NIGHT can be kind or it can be hateful. When Cecy woke next morning Snippy was skipping around her bed, the glorious sun was streaming in windows free from drawn shades, and Miss Benedict was laughing lightly. So the night before had been kind, providing deep sleep and a pleasant awakening. Nothing had happened. No more blazing eyes had followed Cecy, not even in dreams.

Calling good morning, Miss Benedict soon appeared in the doorway swathed in her deep blue robe and looking quite handsome without those hideous glasses. She had not been wearing them often lately.

"And nothing happened," she said with a mocking smile. "You were right, dear. We'll just pretend we are scared enough and perhaps nothing else will happen."

On reaching the dining room they were surprised to find Malika was not there. In her place was a smiling middle aged woman who proved to be none other than Peter's wife.

"Peter came after me," she explained to Miss Benedict. "It seems, Malika had to go early to the city on some important business and didn't want to wake you before she left."

"Humph!" exclaimed Miss Benedict. "Important business indeed. And she didn't want to wake us." She paused while Mrs. Peter served the cereal. "That suits me perfectly. Then, this is the day that *we* go to the city, too, Cecy. We'll just cram our food, and Molly, that's your name, isn't it?" Mrs. Peter said it was. "Well, then, Molly, will you please tell Peter to bring the car around in half an hour. Then you, Molly, stay to clear up and lock up. You and Peter will take over the care of the place——"

"But, Miss Benedict," interrupted Molly, "I wouldn't like to do anything to—well—to make Malika mad," she finished, a little anxiously.

"You won't have to. She won't be back until late today, and by that time you will be gone and you'll take little Snippy with you." The little black dog knew his name and instantly sprang up for Miss Benedict's attention. She patted his head. "Don't you worry, Snippy, Molly and Peter will take good care of you; better care than you have been getting around here," she promised. "Maybe nice juicy bones to chew and bury——" Miss Benedict again turned to the more serious subject.

"Of course," she continued, "Malika will come

back for her things, when she finds the place locked up she'll go over for Peter. Then he will come over with her to get her things. Don't worry that she'll stay around here," she reassured Molly. "When I'm gone she will know that what she wants has gone with me."

Cecy was so mystified at this sudden turn in their affairs that Miss Benedict tried to explain.

"Don't look so surprised, Cecy," she turned to Cecy. "With that sort of people we have to do surprising things. We've been ready for some time and this is the very chance I've been waiting for."

But it was indeed surprising. All Miss Benedict had to do was to pick up a few little things and have Peter carry down to the car four bags which were already packed. One of these she was most particular about. It was evidently a sturdy suitcase, well wrapped and concealed in a thick linen cover. She was so particular about this that she would not let it out of her sight, but walked along with Peter to the car as he carried it.

Cecy had her own small bag ready as quickly as the others were handed out, and in less time than any travelers could possibly have made up their minds, got ready, and started off. The big car pulled out of the drive and Peter parked it while he turned back to lock the gates.

In that few minutes Cecy had a chance to call hello to the two girls she had met the day she had come to the queer place, Betty and Janie. They stood by and waved pleasantly, but Cecy knew they were wondering what all the luggage and the big car hurrying off might mean.

Once out of the town and on the broad highway stretching toward New Jersey's busy cities, Miss Benedict settled herself and sighed as if much relieved.

"This is happening sooner than I had planned," she said to Cecy, "but it's just as well, perhaps better." Cecy smiled and nodded. Evidently Peter was being completely trusted for Miss Benedict did not lower her voice and the big car was not a limousine with a glass partition. "You see, my dear," she went on, "the apartment is all ready. I'm not exactly escaping from Malika and her clan, but this is the easiest way. We have a doorman at the apartment and she can be kept out easily there."

"Oh, yes, Aunt Bessie, I do think it is best to get away from her. That trick of fixing that thing up in the bushes to scare me last night was too silly for anything. I wasn't one bit frightened of the burning eyes, it was the person who put them there who might prove dangerous, I knew."

"You're as right as rain. The ghosts can't hurt us but the ghost makers might," declared Aunt Bessie. "People like Malika are used to frightening poor superstitious folk in their own land, but even young girls like you do not scare so easily in our enlightened America. And that's a good thing." She patted Cecy's knee to make it emphatic.

But riding at top speed even in a big auto does not make confidential talking easy. Miss Benedict sank back in her cushions and Cecy watched the lovely summer scene slip away. Then they were riding through a small city well lined with tall, handsome apartment houses. Peter asked the number just to make sure, and soon they turned in to one of the big gray buildings, and drove along the handsomely outlined half circular drive that led to the massive entrance.

"Peter, you hand me this covered bag in my room yourself," Miss Benedict ordered as they stopped. "The others can be brought up by a boy."

In his light gray livery with its gold braid and brass buttons, the doorman stood at attention after opening their car door. The experience was not new to Cecy; her Aunt Isabel had often gone to call on her friends who lived in equally impressive apartments.

But the corridor down to the rear elevator was long and the carpet soft as fur. This was going to be a wonderful place in which to live. In a second she was thinking of Carol and her father coming here to see her. It was only a short drive into their own place in the larger city nearby. Then, what would Rosie say about Cecy actually having "a job" in a place like this? Thinking of the word job, which had lately become permissible even in polite conversation, Cecy wondered if what she was going to do could be called by so important a name as a job.

After going up past a number of floors in the elevator, they walked down a hall to where the boy with the bags stopped. Then the door was opened by the superintendent who had been leading the retinue, composed of Peter, the call boy and the superintendent.

Inside a private hall the boy touched a button and the door swung back, opening into their own apartment.

"Oh!" Cecy exclaimed, "isn't this lovely!"

The handsome living room was done in shades of yellow and to Cecy seemed gloriously golden. The effect was heightened by lights picking up the color of the walls, decorated in soft yellow tints, and from the windows hung with golden draperies.

"Now, Peter," Miss Benedict was almost whispering "put that bag—Let me see, where. Here, this is my room and this is Cecy's." She had stopped at the door of Cecy's room.

"Aunt Bessie," ventured Cecy, "if you are so careful of that bag wouldn't it be safer here, if this is to be my room?"

"Yes. Exactly. No one would expect—Here, Peter. Right in here." She stood before Cecy's closet. "There, finally, that's that, as they say. At least let us hope so. Cecy, I'll just turn the key in your closet door. Here you take care of it," and she handed Cecy the key. "Well, what do you think of this place?" she asked a moment later.

But whatever Cecy thought of it no one seemed to have time to hear. The other bags were coming in, the superintendent wanted to explain about the row of electric buttons in their hall, then he wanted to tell some one, so he finally decided upon Cecy, what to do about the kitchen electrical appliances. There were so many details to be explained, Cecy was wondering if, after all, an old-fashioned moving were any worse.

Finally the uniformed man was going, but he must have doubted his new tenants intelligence, for he came back again to warn anyone who might listen, that the electric range should never be left on except when in actual use, because electricity for heating purposes was very expensive, much more so than for lights or even for radio, vacuum or other motor uses, he insisted politely.

Cecy assured him she understood, and he finally seemed to believe her.

"Now, Peter, sit down a few minutes. I must be sure you know what you are going to do about the country place," ordered Miss Benedict. Peter sat down. "Molly may be finished with her clearing up by the time you get back, so you can see about the

locking up of everything. Be careful about the barn.
There's nothing important out there but I don't
want any tramps making sleeping quarters of it."

"I know, Miss Benedict. I just had the lock fixed
last week. It was rusty but it's all right now,"
Peter told her.

"That's fine. Now when you're ready to leave
the place, phone that old fellow, what's his name?"

"Squire Hinds?"

"That's the man. Tell him to take over watching
the place and not to let anyone in there. He knows
about Malika and he won't let *her* in, I'm sure of
that." Miss Benedict stopped and brushed her
handkerchief over her face. The day was getting
warm and she had been hurrying. Cecy had already
unpacked her small bag and put her things in the
dresser. She was now, by signs and without interrupting, asking Miss Benedict if she should unpack
the bag she had helped pack for her, the one with
her last things which were hurriedly crammed in as
they were leaving.

"Yes, dear, just put them in any drawer," Miss
Benedict was answering. "We'll get our breath
later on."

Peter was standing. "I'd like to get things settled
and be gone before she gets back," he said signifi-
cantly.

"You will. But don't worry. Malika won't

want to meet our Squire Hinds. Maybe it's a guilty conscience but she hates anything like the law," the woman declared pleasantly.

"I know," Peter agreed. "She hates a cop. That first day she came, Jim Harlow was riding by on his motorcycle and she'd like to kill herself the way she ducked in under the fence, barbed wire and all."

"And met the big dogs there," said Miss Benedict laughing. "You see, Cecy, I had two beautiful big German Shepherds, but I had to send them away," she finished without saying why.

"Safer for the dogs," said Peter, and everyone knew what he meant.

In a few minutes he was gone and Cecy was alone with her new friend. She was wondering about the work in this apartment, when Miss Benedict seemed to answer her thoughts.

"You see, dear, this apartment has a general dining room. Or, if we wish, we may have our meals brought up. Just now we may do as we please about that, but soon we will have to do as someone else pleases," she finished mysteriously.

"Someone else? Who, Aunt Bessie?" Cecy asked in real surprise.

"That's the story I have been waiting to tell you, my dear. I did not ask you to live with me to be my own companion; but merely to find out just what sort of girl you might be. I know now and so we have gone through the first part of our arrangements. The next will show you your real position. You are to be a companion to a very charming and very important young girl."

CHAPTER VIII

CECY WAS AMAZED

COMPANION to a young girl! Cecy was amazed at Miss Benedict's announcement. Who could the young girl be? So this was what Miss Benedict had meant when she had told her she would soon have company. And that explained the lovely twin-bed room done in silver and blue that now seemed like a mystic bower there, just off this living room.

Miss Benedict was watching Cecy, an understanding smile lighting up her pleasant face. They were seated in the golden living room where the dome shaped ceiling gave an impression of more space than the room could actually have measured. It was to have these unusual effects, Miss Benedict had explained, that they had taken this apartment so high up.

"It seems to me," the lady was saying, "they get the apartments more and more unhomelike every year. I shall feel as if I were living in a theatre here."

"Or a circus tent," joked Cecy, referring to the big top.

"Exactly," and they both laughed. "And we depend so completely upon buttons. Buttons everywhere. Hope they don't fail us," she finished.

"But it's a marvellous place," Cecy said again. Then she turned such questioning eyes on Aunt Bessie that the lady seemed ready to answer the question that was unspoken but still understood.

"Yes. I know," she began. "You are wondering who the young girl is to whom you are supposed to be a companion; aren't you?"

Cecy merely smiled in reply.

"Well, it's rather hard to explain. But she is a daughter, that is a *legal* daughter of a young woman who is my own godchild. And I am going to take charge of her while her mother—her adopted mother—you know—is away on an important business trip."

"Oh," said Cecy, very inadequately and waiting for further information.

"Yes, Nora, that's the mother, has some very unusual notions about the girl," Miss Benedict went on, "and I can't say I agree with her concerning them, but we'll see. We'll go along as she wants us to, and I have an idea Nora will learn soon enough, that girls should be girls, not snobs."

"Snobs," repeated Cecy, a vague uneasiness taking possession of her. "I'm afraid I should not be able to—to be good company for a girl who would be snobbish, Aunt Bessie," she finally said.

"Oh, but she's adorable. That's the queer part of it," declared Aunt Bessie. "It's all so unreal. Only a few years ago she was the sweetest little thing, so unaffected, so simple and so lovely. But how she has changed! Everything about her is artificial. And I can't tell whether it's her fault or Nora's," she sighed, plainly unhappy about it all.

"But really, Aunt Bessie, you know I'd do anything reasonable for you," spoke up Cecy with sudden resolve, "but I can't imagine even trying to like a girl who might be, as you say, snobbish."

"Darling," there was entreaty in the word, "just wait until you see her. Perhaps I'm an old fusser, and maybe Sylvia is merely the product of too much pampering. That and the sudden change."

"Change?"

"Yes, indeed. She was once a poor little girl." Miss Benedict had lowered her voice. "It's really a Cinderella story but you are not supposed to know that. In fact, I'm sorry this minute I told you what I just did tell you. It may put too much strain on you to pretend you don't know what you may easily guess."

"Oh, no, don't worry about that," Cecy assured her. "I really can keep my own secrets, Aunt Bessie. But if a girl is, well, you know snooty, we call it, I just couldn't bear her," Cecy declared firmly.

"Now, I know I shouldn't have said that about

Sylvia. I do so want you two to be friends, and I've given such a great account of you to Nora," she admitted. Cecy wondered when all the long distance calls to this Nora could have been made, for she felt sure there had been little time for letter writing to give the account. She was sorry too, to see the anxious expression on her friend's face.

"I want to help Nora because she has gone through a great tragedy and I feel I can help her, perhaps," again Miss Benedict attempted to explain. "She had a darling child of her own, named Sylvia. She was only three years old when she died. The child was almost drowned in a little pool on their own place," she sighed, "and did not get over it."

"How dreadful!" exclaimed Cecy.

"Yes, and this girl, now adopted and strangely called Sylvia after the baby, actually jumped off a roof trying to save the child. She dragged her out and had a doctor there while others were too stunned to move quickly enough. But the baby died of pneumonia," she finished sadly.

"And wasn't the girl hurt from jumping off the roof?" Cecy asked.

"Indeed she was. They had to keep her in a hospital flat on her back for months," Aunt Bessie answered. "But she has entirely recovered now. Of course, Nora loves her and is bravely trying to regard her as the child her own might have become."

"And of course the girl too is trying to fulfill all that," ventured Cecy. "I can understand now why she should want to be the other Sylvia."

This sad story changed the whole picture. Cecy saw at once that she could not let her own pride spoil such plans as those made by Aunt Bessie's friends, Nora and Sylvia. The girl might just seem snobbish because she was trying to follow this new pattern set out for her. Surely it would be explained some way.

"I'll do all I can, Aunt Bessie," Cecy said now, "to help out as you want me to. The reason I hesitated was because I had just gotten used to you, and I wasn't sure how I would get along with a strange girl."

"I know. Perhaps I should have told you at first," Miss Benedict admitted, "but that Malika's treachery and the threats that man made the very day after you came, just upset me so, I couldn't think straight. I have to tell you about that too," she promised. "But now, that we're safe here, it can wait. Oh, dear me! Perhaps I am undertaking too much," she worried, "but I feel sure with your help I can at least *try* to help Nora. She's so set on this plan and she so needs my help with it."

"You can count on me as far as I can go, Aunt Bessie. Be sure of that. They say I make friends easily, and just chumming around with a girl can't be so hard, can it?" Cecy asked simply.

"That's the very thing that drew me to you; you do make friends quickly." The compliment was certainly sincere. "And while Sylvia may be a little hard to understand at first, you, with *your* head and heart, will reach her if anyone could."

"Say, Aunt Bessie," Cecy began cautiously. "You know you are like a different person without those horrid dark glasses."

Miss Benedict put her hands to her eyes and looked quite serious for a few moments, then she smiled broadly.

"That was part of the Egyptian plot," she said. "I did have a little trouble with my eyes when I was traveling around, and the glare of the desert is enough to blind one, so I saw a doctor there. Of course, he ordered my eyes shaded. It was that doctor who started these spies after me and to pretend at least that I was following his advice, I stuck to the glasses."

"Did Malika know this doctor?" asked Cecy instantly interested in the desert mystery.

"Oh, yes. She worked around his place. Seemed like a slave to him, and she seems even now to be sworn to carry out his orders. The contact here is probably through merchants in Cairo who have offices in New York City," Miss Benedict declared.

"Merchants?" Cecy asked.

"Yes. Men who sell all sorts of antiques and curios. Well, I've had enough of antiques," she admitted "and they have gotten me into plenty of trouble. Look out for that bag. That's what the whole band are after, but they'll never get it from me. It is mine, I bought it and paid for it, and none of their threats, nor the curses they declare will follow me if I don't give it back to them, will ever get it away from me," Miss Benedict declared, her voice betraying the emotion that the telling of even that much of the mystery stirred in her.

"That's what's in the bag in my closet?" Cecy said gently.

"Yes. Don't think it's anything dangerous like a python or some charmed snake," Miss Benedict said, "it's nothing but an old moth eaten shawl."

"Just a shawl! And they follow you clear to America for that?" Cecy exclaimed in surprise.

"Yes. They have some reason for wanting it that they do not intend me to know about, I'm sure of that," Aunt Bessie went on, "and I don't believe it is entirely a matter of their religion, as they pretend it is, either. You see, they work for years and years upon a certain kind of prayer shawl. They use it in their temples and have all sorts of rites connected with it, and when I caught a glimpse of this one in an old shop on the road from Cairo to the pyramids, I picked it up at once. For a while nothing happened, then they were on my trail and they've been after me ever since," Miss Benedict sighed, and Cecy went to the refrigerator to get her a cool drink.

"Don't think about it any more today, Aunt Bessie," Cecy pleaded with her. "You are all tired out from our hurried trip and you ought to rest. Come on, take your things off and just lie down," she urged. "It's so easy to run this place you can just leave me with the buttons. If I don't get the right one first time I'll just push another, like my typewriting. I usually have to try a lot of those buttons before I get my words spelled out," she joked.

"All right, dear. I do feel a little exhausted. You see, that bag with the shawl has been a regular nightmare to me for months, and now that you've got it I hope it won't give you any nightmares, Cecy."

"Don't fear, it won't; when the burning eyes in the night-blackened bush didn't bother me, a mere suitcase in my closet, surely won't," Cecy insisted.

But she didn't know the difference then between a mere trick played upon her and the real tragedy of an antique Indian shawl.

CHAPTER IX

SHAWL OF A PRINCESS

ONCE started on the story of the old shawl, Miss Benedict was so stirred up about it she wanted to tell Cecy more of its history, as it had brought its strange influence into her own life.

"The day I got the shawl," she began again, now lying comfortably on her bed while Cecy tried not to move around much, "I had had a sad letter from Nora. You see, she is an important actress and just had to go on with her work," she explained.

"I was wondering what I could get for her and it was my last day in Cairo. I went into one of the old shops on the road to the pyramids, and as usual the merchant showed me his rugs, and his shawls, and all the glittering trashy stuff they try to palm off on tourists. I didn't want any of that and he knew I didn't, but they always make a great show of keeping back something very precious and very special. They do that, of course, to emphasize its value."

Cecy thought she heard someone at the door, and went to find out, but upon going into the hall and listening again there was no buzzer sound, so she quietly returned to where Aunt Bessie was resting.

"Have you ever read up on the hand work of the Orientals?" Aunt Bessie asked.

"We had a little of it in school last year," Cecy replied, "and I thought it fascinating. We studied how they get their dyes from dried bodies of insects, or plant roots. I remember that the rug makers go to the forest to get the bugs for that lovely cochineal crimson, and they dig them out of the bark of the oak trees," she finished quite learnedly.

"Yes, and they can't get the color out of any bug, either," added Aunt Bessie, "only from the female. And now hold your breath. Here's one of those uncountable figures that go into the making of rugs and shawls. It takes fifty thousand bugs boiled in special vats and then dried in the sun to produce *one* pound of dye."

"Whew!" gasped Cecy. "No wonder the dyes last so long. They should. There's an eternity put into their making. I really mean an eternity, as compared to our reckoning of work and time."

"You are right there," Aunt Bessie agreed. "And in the number of knots they use in tying the rug, weaving it on their handmade looms. There's another brain blasting figure. A good Persian Kashan rug has as many as forty thousand to fifty thousand knots in every square foot."

"Oh, yes, I remember about the Kashan rugs," Cecy chimed in. "It was in Kashan that the most famous of all rug makers lived four hundred years ago. He made the 'Ardebil Carpet.' His name was Maksoud and he spent his entire life making that one carpet."

"You learned your lesson well that day," Aunt Bessie complimented Cecy. "I have seen that Ardebil Carpet in the Victoria and Albert Museum in London. It has the maker's name woven in one corner, the name and the rug both immortal."

"You must have been completely overcome to have seen such a wonder, Aunt Bessie," said Cecy, "It just seems as if people become endowed with very different gifts than those we possess, when they devote their lives to them—I mean to get them so perfect."

"That's just it. They did devote their lives to one purpose. And it being an art, and so giving them a chance to develop their own talents, they were satisfied."

Cecy, although no junior philosopher, found something to think about in such astounding historical facts as these.

"But I would rather have a little bit of many things, I think," she added reflectively "than just one rug eating itself into my mind and eyes during my whole lifetime."

"I would, too, although when travelers first come upon these precious things they feel they would give much, too much, to own even the trifling samples," said Aunt Bessie. "That was what led me astray. I was telling you how I got the Kashmir shawl, the strange thing that has eaten into *my* life with its untracable artistry, and to be truthful I'll add, its baneful influence."

"Oh, yes. The shawl that is in the case in my closet. Isn't it strange that we should have one of those pieces that so many hands, and years went into the making of?"

"Isn't it? Well, I'll tell you a little about how I got that. As I said, I had received a sad letter from Nora that day and I was all keyed up over the beauties of these Kashmir shawls. Fifty years ago they were used here in the United States as ladies' shawls, but of late they are only considered wall or museum pieces. So I started out to get one for Nora," Aunt Bessie recited.

"I was about ready to go home when I went looking for a shop, and I found one on the road to the pyramids outside of Cairo, as I was telling you. The Bedouins keep these shops, they are like the gypsies out there. They wear long black cotton robes and winders around their heads and look the part they play, Gypsy merchants of the desert.

"Remember I was telling you how this old fellow

was showing me a lot of trash which he knew I didn't want? But that's the way they lead you on," Aunt Bessie explained.

"They build up," put in Cecy.

"Exactly. Well, after a lot of 'build up' the old fellow went to a shelf in the back of his shop and carried out a shawl so gingerly, holding it flat across his brown hands as if it were crystal instead of a bit of wool. His face beamed and his eyes glittered as he began to show it to me. At that moment the cowbell on the door jangled and he laid the shawl down before me as he went to answer."

Cecy was breathless. All this talk of the Orient was like a play unwinding before her, here in this new elaborate place with a lovely lady telling the story.

"Somehow I had an eerie feeling as I opened that shawl," she said. "It was very fine, with stitches too fine for our ordinary eyes to estimate, embroidered into the most wonderful designs. I was opening it carefully when suddenly I came upon another shawl folded inside." She paused.

"That was the shawl!" Aunt Bessie exclaimed. "It was so exquisitely different, with such a beautiful pattern, you could call it exquisite in its enchanting beauty. I would take that. I did. When the merchant came back I enquired the price and paid it. It was folded up gladly, for the man had had no haggling with me over the price."

"Do you suppose he had not intended to sell you that one?" asked Cecy.

"No, evidently not, although at the time I merely thought he was giving me my choice. I had no idea that one shawl was hiding another," she explained.

"And that," she went on, "was where all the trouble began. I had taken the shawl, and was on my way to the steamer at Alexandria, when frantic messages began to arrive. They must have that shawl back. It was priceless and I don't know what all they claimed for it. But I paid no attention to their demands. When I got to America the New York end of the syndicate began working. That's how Malika came to me. She was sent to follow me on the steamer and would you believe it, Cecy, she actually got me to hire her before I realized she was one of that tribe."

"I have heard those people are wonderfully clever," Cecy said, "and it seems to me a good thing we are here with all the electric buttons and the uniformed guards around us, or they might go on tracing their old shawl."

"That's one reason why I came here; that and to take care of Sylvia for Nora," Aunt Bessie sighed. "But how am I ever going to dare give Nora the shawl that was wrapped around an Indian princess when she was martyred?" she said with a tolerant smile.

"Oh, we'll even find a way to do that," promised

Cecy, more and more interested in the strange story of the sacred shawl and the Bedouin merchant's quest of it. "It must be more than a mere shawl though," Cecy reasoned. "For they could easily get another that would at least look like this one. And to think it's safe in my own closet," she finished lightly.

"Yes," sighed Aunt Bessie, "and you're welcome to it. I'd like a good night's sleep without it being within my reach."

"You think it really was wrapped around an Indian princess when she was martyred?" Cecy asked next.

"There was a bit of paper pinned to it, and while I wouldn't take the shawl out of my trunk while I was traveling, I ventured to show an Arab, who was employed on the steamer, that bit of paper. He interpreted it as declaring the old shawl was a sacred relic centuries old, from the tomb of a beautiful Indian princess, who had been martyred because she would not give up her sweetheart for the favor of a king. He told me the merchant put those stories in with their goods to make them seem more valuable, but said it was a very ancient tag, and to hold on to it. I never told him just what the tag really belonged to and of course he didn't know they were trying to get the shawl away from me," Aunt Bessie made clear.

"It was curious, wasn't it, how you really thought

he was selling it to you and it was only one shawl hidden in the other?" Cecy reasoned.

"Well, thinking it over since, I can see that it was all very curious. Maybe that man wanted to get rid of it and didn't dare sell it, but sort of hoped to lose it. It may have been hidden in his shop by a gang, just as we hear of gangs doing all sorts of terrible things here when poor helpless shop keepers get into their power," Miss Benedict went on. "At any rate, I bought it and paid for it, and the secret way they began searching for it, putting spies along my trail and sending code messages, made me believe those who were after it had no right to it."

"They might have enquired officially, I suppose, if they were honest?" Cecy said.

"Certainly. They could have reached me by the ship's wireless or afterwards in New York City by regular cables to the officials, instead of sending sneaks around like that fellow who came the other day, and even keeping Malika all keyed up to her tricks of trying to scare me into giving it up," declared Aunt Bessie indignantly.

"I think you were very brave, just the same, and I'm sure there is more to it all than just the legend of the Indian princess," Cecy pondered. "Suppose it should really turn out to be priceless, and when the rightful owner discovers what has happened to it, you might be made a princess for returning it."

"Oh, you romantic youngsters!" exclaimed the

lady on the bed. "Next you'll be having an Indian Prince come over the clouds from the Sahara Desert, to claim the shawl of the beautiful young princess who died so long ago————"

"And reward you handsomely," put in Cecy. "Maybe even asking you to go back with him and take charge of his household————"

"Now, darling," interposed Aunt Bessie, "I really couldn't do that. I could use money, and that's no joke, but I just couldn't undertake to manage an Egyptian castle."

They had a good laugh over the story that had seemed to compose itself, but from it Cecy felt she had learned something about Miss Benedict's financial affairs. She *could* use money, and that would help explain why she was doing this for her friend and godchild, Nora, the actress. She was managing, or undertaking to manage, this little home which was by no means a castle, but would probably be just as important to the American princess Nora, and her adopted daughter Sylvia.

The buzzer buzzed and Cecy went to answer it. She felt a little trembly as she put her hand on the door to open it. All their talk of weird desert places and their people, left a disquieting feeling, sort of interrupting reality.

But it was only the superintendent, Mr. Scott.

"Sorry to disturb you," he began " but I wanted to be sure you understand about the refrigerator."

"Oh, yes, Mr. Scott," Cecy smiled, wondering when he would ever be sure that they did understand about all those electric buttons.

"You see, this one is set differently," he explained pointing to one button set in a glass disk in a metal plate with the others. "That's the one that operates the little vestibule in front of the refrigerator," he told Cecy.

"Oh, it operates that glass door in the pantry?" she asked.

"Yes, that's it. And if you should ever get shut in there—I'll show you how to get out."

He led her through the little corridor that led to the kitchenette, then he opened the leaded glass door that brought them in front of the handsome refrigerator.

"You see, now. I'll close this." He allowed the door to swing closed noiselessly. "Now, right here in this black block," he pointed to a block in the tiled floor, "is a little button you just press with your foot." He pressed the almost invisible button and the door swung open magically. "So you never need be afraid of being locked in here," Mr. Scott concluded, gliding out himself as noiselessly as the other contrivances of this very modern and very convenient up-to-date apartment.

When Cecy returned to Aunt Bessie she was almost asleep, "snoozing" as she put it.

"Now, dear, we'll rest awhile and you can call

your sister and tell her all the news," she directed
Cecy. "And if you like you can go in to see them
this evening or they can come out to see you. I'll
take care of the phone. Peter may call, and I guess
you'll be glad to have a little time to yourself."

"Oh, thanks, Aunt Bessie, I would love to take
the bus down home, if you're sure you'll be all right
alone?" Cecy accepted.

"I'll be as safe as if I were in jail," she said jokingly, "what with the bars on the windows and the
uniformed men around, it is sort of jailish, isn't it?"

CHAPTER X

MEET BOBBIE ELLIS

WHAT a relief! Cecy was telling Carol on the phone that she would be home in time to go to the movies.

And Carol was saying: "Sis, I've got the nicest boy for you, a friend of Ken's small brother."

"A small brother, for me?"

"Oh, not too small, just cute," Carol was answering.

"Cute! Carol Duncan! You know how I hate cute boys."

"Oh, he isn't too cute. Just—well, wait till you see him. Only—" she paused, "be sure to be awfully nice to him for he's the brother of Ken's best friend."

"I see. And Ken's your best friend so little sister Cecy——"

"Now listen, dear." The banter of the two sisters was typical of the good times they always had together. "He really is nice, freckles and all, and by name Bobbie Ellis, isn't that—no, not cute, but interesting?"

Cecy finally gave in and admitted it sounded wonderful and that she could hardly wait. As a matter of fact, the few hours now intervening before she would be free to leave Aunt Bessie, did drag heavily. Later the question of Sylvia's coming was again discussed.

"So Sylvia will be here tomorrow," Aunt Bessie was telling her, as they had finished their dinner which had been brought up from the dining room, and Cecy was making final preparations for her bus ride down home.

"Oh, I do hope—she'll like me," Cecy murmured. "You know how queer we girls are, Aunt Bessie."

"But she would be queer indeed if she didn't like you, dear," the woman replied with unmistakable sincerity.

Looking in her mirror, Cecy wondered. Not as pretty as Carol, she was thinking, but not bad. Her light hair, that used to be mousie, was now definitely ash blond, and her eyes, once the family's great worry, were strong and vivid now and no longer needed glasses. Besides that, she was rather tall; winsome, Carol called her, although her best friend, Rosie Wells, always called her slithery.

But, all in all, Cecy Duncan was a very *chic* young girl, and this evening in her new tan silk sport frock, she looked all right. She herself admitted that to the strange mirror.

A squashy little beret, same beige shade as her

dress, topped off the costume, and the snappy pigskin handbag Aunt Isabel had given her last thing, made everything all right.

"My window is closed and locked, Aunt Bessie," she said in leaving. "You know there's a fire escape just below."

"Oh, is there? I hadn't noticed that," said Aunt Bessie, just a trifle apprehensively.

"Oh, it ends on the floor below or in between, I guess," Cecy reassured her. "You know, you're supposed to drop *down* but you couldn't very well drop *up*."

"Of course, dear. And your closet door is locked."

"And the key safe, I won't even say where lest the walls should hear me," whispered Cecy.

She was so happy to be going home, to see Carol and her father, and who could blame her? A job is not a picnic or it couldn't be a job, and being away from home was no fun either.

"Sure you'll be all right, Aunt Bessie?" she was repeating for want of something more important to say.

"Right as rain, darling," Aunt Bessie was always so sort of breezy in her remarks, it kept her from seeming the least bit old. "And you know Katherine Baily is coming to see me. You may stay over night if you want to, I'm sure Katherine would be glad to stay with me."

"Oh, no thank you. I'll be back tonight and not too late either. My sister's friend has a car, if it still runs."

Yes, she would be back that night. To stay at home might weaken her resolve to work this vacation, for Carol and her father both would be sure to urge her to give it up and have some fun. No, she wouldn't risk that temptation, nor would she willingly run right into the confidence Carol would evoke without the slightest intention of doing so. She must keep the Indian shawl story a dead secret, and it might be best to treat Sylvia's coming, as just a young girl going to spend the summer with Miss Benedict.

Just over the hill in the bus to Newkirk, the city seemed a very short distance away. It was so much nicer, really, to be there than out in the woods. In just no time she was at home.

"Darling! Dash in but look out for the smoker; I was just dusting it. How fine you look," and the sisters were in each other's arms, Carol putting the smoker out of harm's way with a deft back hand stroke.

"It seems ages," sighed Cecy. "But that's because it has all been so different. If I started now and kept on prattling I wouldn't have it half told when school opens."

"Now listen, Sis . . ."

"Now you listen, Sis. It's perfectly grand and

I'm having nothing short of a swell time, and I love it! So *please* don't try to change my so-called mind about this job. I wouldn't give it up for a trip out to the Catskills to see Rosie, so there."

"Oh, all right," sighed Carol, taking off the pink smock that had looked so well on her. "Go ahead, and more power to you. And, whisper!" she said. "We're going to send Dad on his fishing trip with the extra dividends."

So they "went into one fit after another," as Cecy would have told it, and one might have thought their separation had been long and arduous. When their father came in he, too, attempted to talk his younger daughter out of her resolve to keep the job, but he was answered by a smothering of kisses that threatened his new glasses and his venerable neck.

To keep the real secret of her new experiences far enough back in her mind, so that it couldn't accidently crop out and tell itself, Cecy began at once to ask about mail—yes, there was a letter from Jimmie Gordon for her—and one from Aunt Isabel.

"And what about this cute little boy I am to take by the hand?" she asked Carol, quickly as she could get a new question in.

"Now be nice to him, Sis, he's the younger brother of Ken's chum, and he has been here two weeks and he needs a little fun."

"I do too," Cecy admitted, "so don't worry. I'll

go after it. His name is Bobbie Ellis? That's easy to remember. Just one more Bobbie that is-all-is."

When Carol's friend Kenneth Powell, Ken to you, came whistling up the stairs there was the echo of a lighter step following. Bobbie's, of course. Cecy pulled a funny face and Carol shook an admonitory finger at her.

"Well, here we are! 'L'ow there, sister? How's the job? This is Bobbie Ellis, Kee-Kee Duncan, Bobbie," and so Ken had taken prompt care of the informalities with a mere wave of his hand. He always called Cecy Kee-Kee.

Bobbie was nice; in his blue flannel jacket and his white ducks, with his hair brushed into submission apparently by a determined hand, although a couple of fish hooks had escaped to his forehead making him look more Bobbyish and perhaps "cute," as Carol had meant it. Without the least embarrassment he crossed the room and sat beside Cecy on the small divan.

"Glad to meet a girl who still goes to school," he began. "I get sort of fed up with all these experienced folks." He had lowered his voice and was smiling toward Carol and Ken, who were already too busy with their own affairs to be noticing the youngsters.

"But I'm a working girl now," Cecy answered the boy with the shadows under his big brown eyes; freckles, likely, in daylight.

"Working girl?"

"Didn't Carol tell you? I've got a real job, my first, I've got to admit."

"At what, for gosh sakes?"

"I'm not sure whether I'm in the secret service or on the police force——"

"Oh, one of those girl stunts, eh?" he sort of scoffed.

"No, it is not. It's a real job," insisted Cecy, "No silly girl stunts, if that's what you mean."

"I didn't really. But I guess we're going." He stood up with easy good manners. "Hope the movie won't be a bed-time. All I've seen since I came down here are factories and kid movies."

"Now, Bobbie," smiled Cecy, "we'll have to get you over to New York. The factories, of course, are here in New Jersey."

"Here we go," called out Ken. "Come along, babes."

"Dad, we'll be back," Carol was saying to her father.

"I won't," Cecy announced. "I've got to be out on Northfield Road by eleven."

"Cecy, can't you stay tonight?" Carol implored.

"Not tonight, darling, some other night. Good-bye Dad. Don't work too hard, but you do look fine." She was kissing him and patting his gray hair into the place where it would never stay put, on the crown of his handsome head.

At the movie Bobbie and Cecy managed to get in considerable conversation, because seats directly back of them were not occupied. Both of them seemed eager for a chance to talk, Cecy finding the boy frank and unaffected, and Bobbie simply delighted to have a real girl like Cecy to talk to.

"Now, listen, Cece," he said suddenly, by coining a nickname showing his liking for her, "What do you mean, work? Why can't we go out riding afternoons? Jim lets me take his car——"

"You have a license?"

"Of course," he replied largely, as if Cecy might easily have known he had had a sixteenth birthday a month ago and had got his license that very day.

"That's fine," Cecy said quickly. "But honest, Bobbie I *do* work."

"Well, suppose you do. There's the labor laws," he pointed out. "You've gotta have a whole day every week; haven't you?"

Cecy started to giggle so uncontrollably that Carol got hold of her arm and squeezed it.

"Have a good time," she whispered, "but don't annoy the animals."

"What's funny about the labor laws?" demanded Bobbie on the other side of her.

"They are," hissed Cecy. "Me and the labor laws!"

"That's just what I think, so let's go riding——"

A sudden sharp thought cut through Cecy's mind.

This Sylvia person; what would she be like? What would please her? Maybe Bobbie would. Maybe she would like to go riding with this nice boy and with Cecy, herself, of course. That might be a good way to break through this snob business.

"All right, Bobbie," she whispered, as the movie flashed by, threatening to leave them in total ignorance of its story, "It would be nice if I can arrange it to go out some afternoon. Call me up."

CHAPTER XI

IT WOULD HAPPEN THAT NIGHT

CECY found her Aunt Bessie's light still on when she got back to the apartment, after the enjoyable evening with Bobbie Ellis at the movies, so she went to the door to speak to her.

"Still awake, Aunt Bessie? Not too excited to sleep. I hope?"

"No, my dear, but—maybe you are?" said the good-natured lady, pointedly.

"I? Why?"

"Because your eyes are dancing and your cheeks are blooming. But that's as it should be. You ought to go home and have a time with your young folks as often as you can. You're entitled to it."

Bobbie and the labor laws, thought Cecy. If he could hear Aunt Bessie he would likely get her to form a little labor union of his own, with the one and only law, that of letting girls work merely once in a while.

"Oh, yes, I did have a lovely time," Cecy admitted needlessly. "Were you all right?"

"Perfectly. Katherine didn't come. She phoned she would have to be late and I told her not to bother coming as you would be sure to be back. Then Peter phoned. Malika had been there and she got her things and left with scarcely a mutter. You see, dear, Peter had the moral support of his Squire Hinds. And just as Peter said, Malika *don't* like cops."

They laughed at Peter's joke, and Aunt Bessie went on to tell how Malika had so much truck to carry that Peter wouldn't crowd it in his car, so she threw out something that looked like a scare crow, according to Peter. He said it seemed to be a bunch of colored things with a kind of head on it. And he went farther to say that the head was a shower bathing cap with the eye windows in it. He saw the bundle open as she tossed it out."

"The ghost of the burning bush!" exclaimed Cecy, recalling the trick that undoubtedly Malika had tried to play on her the night before they left Tanglewood. "And the rubber cap does have isinglass windows. Dad has one of those caps. That's how she was able to put a light in for eyes," Cecy was positive.

"Well, Peter says she was mad as hops," Aunt Bessie went on, "and, of course, we haven't seen the last of her. Worse luck."

"But you do feel we are pretty safe here, don't you?" Cecy asked a little anxiously.

"Oh, yes, of course I do. In fact, who could get past all our buttons and the guards in uniform? So, don't let's worry, although we can't help being a bit jumpy, I suppose," Aunt Bessie admitted, shifting around on the strange bed that seemed made for her personal comfort.

"Hasn't it cooled off beautifully?" Cecy remarked. "Look at your curtains ballooning out like a blimp ready to take off. I'll go get you a nice glass of cool milk, and then I suppose we had better get settled for the night."

"Wait just a minute, dear. I would like the milk and we should get settled, but first let me tell you something. You know our Sylvia comes tomorrow."

"Yes," said Cecy crisply, "tomorrow is the day."

"And I know everything is going to be all right, that you two girls will get on famously."

The way she said that made Cecy suspicious. What she meant was, plainly, that she hoped they would get along, admitting doubt as to the situation.

"I'll do my best——"

"You needn't tell me that. But I've been thinking it all over, and it seems to me, it would be best to be just what we seem to be, friends," said Aunt Bessie. I'll be a friend of your Aunt Isabel's——"

"You mean I would have to pretend not to be working for you?"

"No, you wouldn't have to. I know you are highspirited and proud to be working. But you know, Cecy darling, sometimes we are obliged to use business strategy."

Cecy was sitting on the low bedside chair, twisting her beret into impossible shapes. She brought her head up suddenly now, like a colt ready to break away.

"But why the strategy?" she asked, sorry as always to oppose her friend. "How can we ever get anywhere through deceit?"

"I know, I know," Aunt Bessie turned down her light until the shade was a mere tint of pink. "But it is a long story and, well, as a matter of fact, I am a friend of your Aunt Isabel's," she said finally.

"You *do* know Aunt Isabel?"

"Yes. I've written her a few times and she has answered. I know her as well through those letters, and better perhaps, than if I had played bridge with her through many stupid afternoons. I hate bridge."

"How did you get her address?" Cecy asked hesitantly.

"Oh, you see, dear, her name was given by the agency in reference, besides your family's name here."

"Of course," Cecy recalled. "You would like Aunt Isabel," she added.

"I do. She has a woman's heart and a man's will. And she was simply delighted that you had struck out on your own. So now, I'm your Aunt

Bessie, adopted, and I am a friend of your family's. That will make it much easier. You are with me because I had been alone out there in the country, and so you are going to finish out your vacation here. That's all right. No deception, no subterfuge and —nobody's business," concluded the lady under the pink coverlet, beside the pink lamp and along the window with the billowing pink hangings.

"I'll get the milk," Cecy said, just a trifle dejectedly. She was very glad she had had the good time with Bobbie Ellis tonight. After all, young folks must stick together.

Out into the small kitchen she went, releasing the door that had the secret spring that would have operated by a hidden button if the door had been locked which it had not been. Cecy just put her hand to the refrigerator door that automatically turned on a light in the box, when a scream, a terrifying scream cut through the place.

"Oh, Aunt Bessie!" she called, "what is it. What happened?"

In an instant she was back in the bedroom where Aunt Bessie continued to scream and call for help.

"Oh, the window! Don't go near it!" the distracted woman begged. "Call someone! Quick."

"But—there's no one there, Aunt Bessie," Cecy said quickly, going toward the open window. "Just the curtains blowing."

"But I saw it, right in the center, between the two

drapes. Call someone. Touch a button; you know which one. Don't let that terrible creature escape and maybe get in here later."

She was so breathless, and so terrified it was impossible to find out what had happened, but Cecy felt sure she had merely been frightened by something outside, perhaps nothing menacing at all.

"Just wait, Aunt Bessie," she begged. "You're all in a perspiration. I'll get the milk this time——"

"No, no. Don't go out there again. I tell you there was a hideous face at that window. Cecy, please call somebody. We must have that little balcony around the window searched," she insisted.

Without a moment's loss of time Cecy had gone to the kitchen again, and was now back with the glass of milk.

"Here, dear Auntie," she coaxed "just drink this. You're all tired and nervous. I shouldn't have gone out and left you this evening. There, that's right. Drink it all, and let me sponge your face."

"But he'll get away!" protested the frightened woman, who really had finished the milk and was now allowing Cecy to wipe her face with a cloth dipped in refreshing toilet water.

"Let him get away and good riddance," said Cecy cheerfully. The last thing she wanted to do was to "call out the guards," as she would have expressed it, on this, their very first night at Winston Arms.

In snatches of sentences she finally managed to give that idea to Aunt Bessie, but the still frightened lady was not easy to convince.

"It's cool enough now to close your window and pull down the blind," Cecy was saying, as she very bravely went over to the other side of the bed to perform those tasks. She was wondering, of course, what really had happened, but was quite satisfied not to go any further than just to the window ledge to find out. There was a small balcony even with the window, but tomorrow would be time enough to explore that.

"Quick, shut it," begged Aunt Bessie. "I don't know when I was as frightened as that. To scream and yell so. It isn't like me," she said in sort of apology.

"Our walls are sound proof," Cecy reminded her pleasantly.

"But the window was wide open——"

"We'll look over our balconies tomorrow; we didn't have time today. But I'm sure it was the wind up to some trick," Cecy speculated. "You see, there are high lights beyond the court out there, and they could easily make faces through your drapes; there are big figures in them, see?" she pointed out, holding a piece of the soft damask out from the window for Aunt Bessie to see the faces it could make, with a strong light behind it.

"Well, maybe. But it did give me a turn."

"Of course it did. I'll leave my door open between," Cecy offered. And she was thinking, of
course, about the Indian shawl in the suitcase in her
closet.

Could Aunt Bessie really have seen someone at
the window? She tiptoed around, anxious to let
the excited woman get to sleep. There were two
closets in her room so she did not have to unlock
the one where the shawl was hidden.

But Aunt Bessie's sudden burst of excited alarm
was really surprising, and hard to understand. She
had seemed so reasonable and coolheaded. Could
she really have seen someone at that window? Or
had the Oriental story telling that afternoon, with
all its old terrors, keyed her imagination up to an un-
controllable pitch?

Strange that she, Cecy, was pretty hard to scare
these days. Perhaps, after all, young girls were
getting the right kind of courage.

Dismissing the face at the window as unworthy
of further speculation, she turned happily to thinking of her own pleasant evening.

"Bobbie was a treat," she was thinking as she
slipped off her things, " and it would have been nice
to be free to enjoy a vacation with him. He was
cute. She had always hated that term applied to
boys but it did seem to suit Bobbie."

When he said as they came out of the movie:

"Good gosh! You don't know how a fellow feels

slinking around with all the smart oldies making faces at him. Of course, Jim is swell, and Ken too, he's just great, and Carol is a peach. But somehow, girls and boys like you and me need our own ages. Don't you think so?"

She did. And even the ghost at the window and the Indian shawl in her closet, and the mysterious Sylvia almost arriving, could not argue against that.

CHAPTER XII

SYLVIA COMES

CECY awoke with that feeling of gloom that follows an unhappy night. It was Aunt Bessie's scare, of course. A scream like that from quiet Aunt Bessie was enough to upset anyone. Cecy was getting up, for *this* was the day. Sylvia was coming, and it was best to be ready, no matter what time it was now or what time she would come. Cecy remembered she was to look over those little balconies around the windows, and also make sure about the general surrounding across the court that separated the tall apartment houses. Next time something like a face should flit across their windows, she was deciding, they might at least guess where it was coming from.

She found Aunt Bessie too interested in the imminent arrival of Sylvia, to even mention events of the night before.

"I've had a 'phone from her school in Connecticut," she told Cecy. "She left very early, so she will be here in the early afternoon."

"Motoring?" Cecy asked, casually.

"Oh, yes. She'll have baggage and is to stop at New Haven for a maid Nora is sending along. She'll do our cooking, you know," said Aunt Bessie, slowly.

And so, very soon the placid, comfortable life that Cecy and Aunt Bessie had just about perfected between them, would be all changed.

A strange young girl and a strange maid were coming upon them like an army of invasion, and Cecy at least, if not Aunt Bessie herself, was now anxiously awaiting the upheaval, or the invasion, whichever it might turn out to be.

"We have been so happy. Aunt Bessie," Cecy said impulsively, as she helped the lady slip her lovely orchid morning dress over her head without disturbing her hair-wave, "I've just got to tell you before we get all mixed up. You see, my sister Carol and I have had no mother for a long time, and Aunt Isabel brought me a sense of real protection. I have felt the same way since I've been with you," she said wistfully.

"My dear," choked Aunt Bessie, "I knew I needed a young girl around me. Gives *me* something to do. And I hope Sylvia will feel the same way about me as you do."

"Do you know her—well?"

"I can't say I do. I've seen her a number of times, of course. But she was always going some place else, to school, to New York to see Nora. Last winter she went down to Atlantic City and stopped over one night— Ah, well," she sighed. "We must be patient with her. The child has had a lot of trouble in her own short life."

The things that happened before Sylvia came seemed of small importance, although Cecy did find a window across the court opposite Aunt Bessie's window, with an unobstructed view, straight over. A flash from the other window would have shown directly into their apartment, Cecy decided, which almost spoiled another scare counting the first one, those burning eyes in the darkened bush.

"But it won't all be as easy as that," Cecy was positive, for the Indian shawl and the Bedouin spies out to get it back, made a sinister threat too real to be played out in silly tricks. There could be no denying that probability.

"Oh," exclaimed Cecy as she heard voices. "She must be coming——"

The buzzer sounded and Aunt Bessie hurried into the foyer to answer it. Realizing that she did not want Cecy to open the door, Cecy stepped back into her own room, her heart fluttering, although she had been determined "not to be silly."

"Oh, Aunt Bessie!" The voice was childishly sweet. Certainly that girl was glad to see Aunt Bessie.

"Sylvia darling!" They must be embracing. Cecy was already feeling shut out, distanced from her Aunt Bessie.

"What a lovely place!"

"Here is your room, dear. The chauffeur will bring in your bags." Aunt Bessie's voice had a little quake in it. Was she, too, nervous of this young girl?

"I'm so glad to get here——"

"Irma," (that must be the maid) "you'll find a small room just off the kitchen. Yes, there," she was walking straight past Cecy's door, "right there. That's right."

It was then that Cecy Duncan felt the difference between being just herself, and being in the position she held. Her cheeks burned. Even her eyes seemed filmed over; not from anger or hurt pride; she was not too proud for this, but from the feeling one girl is so apt to get when another girl overlooks her. The mean little word "snob" was fairly hissing itself at her, but Cecy knew she, herself, was acting and feeling snobbish.

The voices in Sylvia's room had died down to indistinguishable sounds.

"She will resent me being here, I'm sure of that," raced Cecy's thoughts. "That's why Aunt Bessie doesn't call me out."

Not being wanted and being away from home can hurt, and it was hurting Cecy. If only they would

come out or call her; ask for something, or do anything to break this sort of imprisoned feeling that
was working up in her.

Then she heard: "To stay! You said—just
you—" That was Sylvia's voice. And the next
sentence too low to reach into Cecy's room was followed by:

"Oh, Aunt Bessie! I just can't. I want to get
away from girls. I hate them—all!"

Cecy knew then she would have to walk out, now,
to the kitchen or some place, any place so she would
make her presence felt. She moved a chair noisily.
She opened and shut the closet door. Then Aunt
Bessie called:

"Cecy! Come here, dear, I want you to meet
Sylvia!"

The very blond head raised itself from small
hands, as Cecy entered the room, but the girl did not
turn to greet her.

"Sylvia dear, here's Cecy. She's a niece of a
friend of mine in the Midwest, and I don't know
what I should have done——"

The girl turned and faced Cecy. A lovely face
but— There was something familiar about it.

"Did you have a nice trip, Sylvia?" Cecy managed
to say. But the girl must have instantly recognized
her, for she turned pale in spite of her make-up, and
again buried her face in her hands without uttering
a word.

"She does know me," Cecy secretly decided. "But she doesn't look like— Of course, I only saw her a few times." Thoughts flew through Cecy's mind, troubled, unhappy thoughts.

Aunt Bessie was the picture of despair. What could she do to break this tense situation?

"I'll run out and do the marketing, Aunt Bessie," Cecy said merely as an excuse, and the distraught woman nodded gratefully.

As Cecy left the room she heard sobs, bitter, heart breaking sobs. And Aunt Bessie was helplessly offering comfort.

"That was it," Cecy knew. "She is changed, deliberately changed. And that was why Aunt Bessie didn't want anyone from around here. Oh, why didn't I say I used to live in Melody Lane!"

Aunt Bessie was out in the hall going toward her own room, which was on an ell from Cecy's. Instantly Cecy stepped noiselessly to Sylvia's door.

The girl looked up, her face distorted from crying. Cecy put her finger to her lips in a clear sign not to say anything to Aunt Bessie. Startled, Sylvia looked earnestly with those lovely hazel eyes now so tear-spoiled. But she seemed to understand, and nodded slightly.

Back in her own room Cecy snatched up a pad and pencil and wrote. "It's all right. Wait, until I can speak to you." This she quickly tossed into

Sylvia's open door, just as Aunt Bessie made sounds of coming out of her room.

"Oh, Aunt Bessie!" Cecy called cheerfully. "Maybe *you* would like to go out and get some air; I could help Sylvia unpack."

The look on Aunt Bessie's face was one of complete astonishment. "How could Cecy suggest that?" she was saying, without uttering a word.

But they were both in the hall and Sylvia was in her room, so Cecy was making a lot of signs. They meant "Please go out. It will be all right."

Bewildered, but seemingly glad of any chance to change this situation, Aunt Bessie replied:

"All right. I have some papers to sign at the bank. If you and Sylvia will be all right——"

"Of course we will," spoke up Cecy bravely, much more bravely than she felt. But she, herself, was in this and she had to make one grand effort to get out of it. And that's exactly what she was going to do.

Aunt Bessie was plainly anxious about leaving the two girls alone, but Sylvia was now in her bathroom, evidently repairing the lost "make-up" which was so unusual in a girl of her age, and that gave Cecy a good chance to reassure Aunt Bessie.

"Just leave her to me," she whispered. "She'll be all right. She's only a little girl, really——"

"I know. But she's so headstrong——"

But Cecy was literally patting Aunt Bessie out to

get the cab she had called, and now she must face Sylvia.

She had come back into her room from the bath-room.

"May I come in?" asked Cecy. Her voice was friendly but not patronizing.

"If you want to." That voice was not so friendly.

"Can't we be friends, Sylvia?"

"Friends! You told Aunt Bessie you were from the West. You're from Melody Lane!"

"I had just come from the West. Yes, I did live in Melody a few years ago——" Cecy was studying this girl, not sure she was really that little girl who only a few years ago had caused all the excitement in Melody Lane. But she was certainly recognizing Cecy.

"Of course, you can't stay here," the girl snapped.

"Why can't I? Do you realize I am working here and that I need this work?"

"Working here! Aunt Bessie said——"

"I know. She's good and kind and didn't want me to feel I was a——servant. But I am," blazed Cecy. "And if you insist upon making me lose this work——" Her voice choked. She was fighting her own battle now. "I don't have to trouble you or be in your way," she flared again. "Aunt Bessie and I got along wonderfully, and I'm going to stay here if she will let me."

CHAPTER XIII

A HEART-BROKEN GIRL

CECY's determined outburst took Sylvia by complete surprise. After all, she was younger than Cecy, and in spite of her defiance she seemed timid and even afraid. As Cecy looked at her now it struck her *that* was probably the real cause of the girl's obstinacy; she was afraid of something and always ready to defend herself.

As Sylvia sat now on the blue bench before the dainty dressing table, Cecy was struck with her childish beauty. Her hair, in a mass of cupid ringlets, was a shade too golden, and her eyes, round and glinting sparks, agate brown, seemed somehow unnaturally outlined. Her nails finishing off small, pretty hands were too highly tinted with some sort of blended color like glistening shells. But in spite of all this artifice, she was, as Aunt Bessie had said, adorable.

She had changed from the blue traveling suit to a pale orchid chiffon, and while this seemed elaborate for an ordinary summer day, Cecy was thinking how really beautiful its soft, delicate tone made Sylvia look.

But she was not calm, and plainly felt ill at ease, almost awkward, and this lack of poise completely contradicted all her staged effect.

"Why did you say you were from the West?" she charged Cecy. "I didn't want any young girl here. I'm sick of all of them," she said bitterly, "but I know Nora especially ordered Aunt Bessie not to hire anyone from—around here."

"Now please listen, Sylvia." Cecy had sat down on the damask chair. "When I came to inquire about this work, of course, you know Aunt Bessie was out in the country then, I hadn't the slightest idea there was any restriction about where one came from. My reference from the agency stated I had just come from school in the Midwest. This was perfectly true, of course. In fact, I have not lived in the East with Dad and Carol since they came into Newkirk. The West with Aunt Isabel was really my home."

She saw Sylvia put her nails to her lips then quickly draw them down again. She would not consciously bite them, but she was nervous enough to do so if she had not remembered, just in time. And she kept turning her head away from Cecy, and just as persistently she would turn away from the mirror she was facing. Cecy began to pity her, to wish she didn't have to antagonize her.

"Carol?" Sylvia asked. "Your sister is Carol?"

"Yes; do you know her?" Cecy sked. But seeing

this question really agitated Sylvia, she went on with her own story.

"So you see, Sylvia," she went on finally, "when Aunt Bessie said she was glad *I* wasn't from around here, and hurried right on with some other matter I couldn't see why I should drag up Melody Lane after being away from there three years."

"But I've got money: Nora gives me too much. I'd give you more than——than you get here," Sylvia stumbled. "If I could just be let alone."

"Oh, I couldn't take your money," said Cecy proudly. "I'm glad to earn some to help my sister Carol. *She's* been working in a day nursery among poor children, her work is *hard*. Of course, she and Dad didn't want me to do this; I had a hard time to convince them I was determined to work this summer. And now, when it's half over——" Cecy's voice trailed off as discouragement overcame her.

She felt Sylvia's eyes fastened on her now.

"You know me, don't you?" she asked almost in a whisper.

"I thought I did, but I'm not sure now. The little girl I knew was so different." Cecy paused, wondering if she should tell her what she was thinking.

"How different?"

"She was the dearest child imaginable," blurted out Cecy, her voice full of admiration. "She was so kind to others, she had risked her life for a poor little sick boy. And once she climbed up to an attic to reach an old woman," she was saying breathlessly. "That little girl could never get——"

"So hard, so bitter as I am?"

"I don't believe you are either hard or bitter," Cecy felt obliged to contract "but you are threatening to make me lose this work. Why?"

"You *do* know who I am?"

"I thought I did, but you must have changed even in appearance."

"Have I, do you think?" Sylvia's voice rose with hope. She seemed to want dreadfully to have changed.

"As I said, I never saw much of this little girl in Melody Lane," Cecy answered, "but I heard a lot about her."

"Yes, that's it. Everyone *heard* a lot about her. She was that kind of a——kid, she didn't care then what anyone said about her."

"And now——she does?" pressed Cecy.

"Oh, Cecy. You don't know——how hard it all is. How hard I've tried to be someone else, to forget Melody Lane."

A sudden outburst of crying made Cecy feel guilty. She should not have pressed her so hard. Leaving the bench, Sylvia threw herself on the bed and wept like a child, and Cecy was thinking how terrible it would be if Aunt Bessie came back before all this was cleared up.

"I'll tell you, Sylvia," she said very gently. "We both have a secret about each other. I don't know, that is I am not sure who you are. Aunt Bessie told me about your saving Nora Grant's, the actress' baby, but she never mentioned your name even when she told me Miss Grant had adopted you and had so wanted you to take the place of the lost child."

"You—you know that? Then you know, surely you can guess why I have done all this?" sobbed Sylvia.

"Yes, I can. And I can guess a lot more. Maybe some time you will tell me. I'm sure you would feel very different, Sylvia, if you just talked about it."

"Oh, I know I never could," moaned Sylvia. "Even to think about it hurts more and more."

"About what?" asked Cecy, directly.

"About, about, pretending to be someone else. Changing my name, changing my looks—" she was getting excited now, "and giving up everyone I loved! Oh, you don't know how I ache to see them, the darlings that loved me so!"

Again Cecy had to wait until the paroxysm of weeping subsided. She had wet a handkerchief with a fragrant cologne and was offering it to the girl —hoping soon she would be able to stop crying, before Aunt Bessie came.

"I must talk fast, Sylvia," she said. "You and I must come to an understanding before Aunt Bessie comes back. Let me ask you one question. Does Miss Grant know all this? Did she ask you to change your appearance and give up those you love?"

"Oh, no, she wouldn't do that!" protested Sylvia. "But she wanted me to take the place of her own little Sylvia, to be like she would have been."

"Sylvia Grant! That's your name now, isn't it?"

"Yes."

"Well, I believe you are all wrong. That all this changing, and giving up your friends, and actually being someone else is not at all what Nora Grant would want. I know Nora Grant by reputation, not just as an actress, and she is too true a lady to want you to do any of those strange things."

Sylvia was staring at her companion. "But she told me she wanted me to be just as near like—the real Sylvia as I could be," she gasped.

"Yes, exactly. But would that real Sylvia make herself over? Become artificial? And above all, spoil her character by giving up loyal friends?"

The expression of simplicity on the girl's face was pathetic. She turned to face the mirror as she now sat on the bed. She put her hand to her hair; she looked down at her nails, she even took hold of the fine chiffon in her dress, so unlike the simple print in Cecy's. She was taking stock of her appearance. Cecy pitied her.

"That's a lovely dress," she told Sylvia to break the strain.

"Maybe. But not for me. I guess I don't know and I can't learn." Her words dropped like pebbles on hard metal.

"Nonsense. Have *I* made you feel discouraged?"

"Oh, no, I knew it was wrong, all this. But you see—well, the girls went to this beauty shop and they told *me* I ought to go."

"And *that's* why you use—make-up, and you had your hair tinted?"

"Oh, yes I did and I hate it," cried out Sylvia. "My hair was not this color at all."

"But it was light always, wasn't it?"

"Yes, but not this—the beauty parlor girl called it Cupid gold," she said in derision, getting hold of one of her ringlets and giving it a vicious pull.

There was a stir at the door. Cecy had completely forgotten the maid, Irma, she had been so quiet. Yes, it was Irma and Cecy answered her few discreet questions. How different she was from the ever present Malika, Cecy thought.

As Irma left them Cecy pressed for a quick decision on all this strange unfolding of Sylvia's troubles, which so intimately affected herself.

"Sylvia," she said, "we all make mistakes. I made mine when I did not insist upon telling Aunt

Bessie I had one time lived in Melody Lane. But I did not know it was important. Was it Miss Grant who gave that order?"

"Oh, no. Nora would not interfere that way," Sylvia answered. "But, you see, when I decided to spend all that money at the beauty shop and they guaranteed to make me over, they said it would be best for me to give up any friends I used to have. I suppose they just wanted me to be safe from— well, from criticism," she ended lamely.

"But you, Sylvia, can save me from criticism. I know Aunt Bessie would understand my mistake, but somehow, just now until things get straightened out, I wish she didn't have to know."

"I won't tell her, you needn't be afraid," Sylvia spoke up, an expression of something like relief changing almost into a smile.

"Oh, thank you; you don't know what that means to me," exclaimed Cecy. "You see my sister Carol——"

"I know your sister Carol, and she did a lot for me out in Melody Lane," admitted Sylvia at last.

"She has done more for poor children in her nursery in the city," added Cecy. "But now, Sylvia, we have a bond between us. That's the way grown-ups talk, but it's the best word I can think of just now."

"But then, you'll have to help me," Sylvia pleaded.

"Of course I shall. You can't guess all the interesting things I'm dying to tell you about. About a very nice boy, Bobbie Ellis. Do you like to go out riding with nice boys?" she asked, archly.

But Aunt Bessie was coming down the foyer.

CHAPTER XIV

STRANGE MESSENGER

To SEE Aunt Bessie come into the apartment, her arms laden with bundles, topped off by a great bouquet of garden flowers, a hall-boy close behind her carrying all he could possibly manage in the way of things from the market, Cecy, all smiles now and happy after the girls' session, was thinking:

"To see her come in like this is worth the price of admission."

And certainly it was. Consternation in her own expression, as she, Aunt Bessie, made sure the girls' smiles were real and not an act fixed up to please her, was so complete that Sylvia pushed out a chair for her and began unloading the packages, for indeed the surprised lady seemed ready to drop.

"Oh, oh," she sort of murmured. "You girls— all right?"

"Oh, certainly," spoke Sylvia, before Cecy could have done so. "We were wondering what kept you so long."

Sylvia was taking the bouquet out to the kitchen. Irma was busy with the market parcels.

Cecy whispered: "Maybe she thought we'd need flowers," she giggled into Sylvia's ear. At which remark Sylvia, too, got laughing.

As always the reaction from tense anxiety offers the opposite and the two girls now just couldn't help laughing. Even Irma, the imperturbable, looked at Sylvia in amazement.

But it was Aunt Bessie whom Cecy was worrying about. She would have to give her some sort of high sign before she might collapse from her mounting amazement. Once or twice she attempted to ask a question, but Cecy so quickly and so pointedly interrupted her, that she seemed to give up and just sit there in a swoon of relief.

Buzzing around her Cecy managed such remarks as "It's all right, everything's fine." And then aloud to prepare for the next change she asked:

"Aunt Bessie, would you mind if Sylvia and I went down town a little later? She wants to do some shopping."

"Mind! Certainly not. Just call that cabman I've engaged for our regular service. It will do you both good," Aunt Bessie insisted.

"But maybe Bobbie Ellis will call up. You know, Aunt Bessie, you promised we could ride with Bobbie, if Sylvia wasn't too tired," Cecy attempted.

"Oh, I'm not tired," came a new voice from Sylvia "and if we could all go together I'd love—a ride."

Cecy noticed how Sylvia emphasized *all*. Of

course the two girls would go together, if Bobbie
phoned.

Only those who have had to go through so hard a
battle at understanding, as Cecy and Sylvia had run
into that afternoon, can realize what a relief their
understanding was. Calling Sylvia a snob, Cecy kept
thinking, when she was merely scared to death.
Naturally, there was much more to be explained between them than could even be touched upon in that
hour of wild charges, and confused arguments.

But the important point was gained when poor
Sylvia admitted her mistake in trying to make herself over, urged on probably by some clever business
woman operating near her Connecticut school.

"I'll have to go carefully," Cecy was deciding, as
she was putting on her new yellow sweater and the
tan skirt Carol had given her, and Sylvia was trying
to find something among her clothes that might be
suitable for the ride—if Bobbie called.

"And when I tell her about the Indian shawl and
Aunt Bessie's danger," mused Cecy, "I'm sure she
will soon forget herself and jump in to help us with
the mystery. She's been too long and too much
alone. Girls need girls," she was concluding quite
wisely, "and maybe," she was secretly adding,
"sometimes they need boys too. Bobbie Ellis, get
your call in."

As if somebody had actually told Bobbie that
Cecy was trying to send him that secret message,

the phone rang almost immediately and it was he.

Cecy was promptly answering yes, she could go and that she had a surprise for him, a new girl would be going along.

Bobbie had no objection to that, "the more the girlier," he joked, but he knew a nice boy, a summer student at Columbia, and couldn't he fetch him along so they'd be four instead of three.

"Not this time, Bobbie," Cecy answered critically. She could not attempt to explain with Sylvia within hearing, and it was not easy to make the eager boy at the other end of the wire understand why he couldn't bring his friend along.

Finally he gave in, and as Cecy turned away from the phone she found Sylvia beckoning to her to come into her room. The apartment, although the rooms were large enough, did not afford the privacy of a house plan.

Sylvia looked distressed again. She had put on a print dress, evidently a school costume; she had brushed much of the natural curl out of her hair, and had apparently overdone her face scrubbing, for it certainly shone.

"What's the matter, Sylvia?" Cecy asked her anxiously.

"Would you *think* me—mean, if I backed out and didn't go out with you?" Sylvia herself asked very slowly.

"Not go? Why?"

The girl turned away so that Cecy could not see her face. For a minute she did not answer.

"Oh, I don't know," she murmured finally with an escaping sigh. "I thought I could do it, but I'm so mixed up."

"Of course, you are," Cecy quickly agreed. "Who wouldn't be? But the way to get over it, Sylvia, is to get at something else, forget what you have been doing, that is, try to forget it," she finished.

"Cecy, I know you're right, and I'm terribly wrong, but—well, perhaps I can't change so quickly." Their voices were low although Aunt Bessie was probably sleeping. "You see, it took me so long to decide to do all that, that I just can't seem to undo it in a few hours."

Cecy had urged Sylvia into her own room. She must, she knew, help her to conquer this now, or it would be harder when she tried again. Cecy hated to hurt this queer girl, and looking at her there so devoid of make-up and so natural in her school dress, Cecy was again struck with her peculiar beauty, something angelic looking about her, she decided. Of course, it must have been that "look" that had tempted the beauty parlor people to apply their magic.

"Sylvia," pleaded Cecy, "just come along now; we haven't much time, you know. Do that for me, and I promise you I'll do a lot more for you. You can't guess what you and I have to do right here for Aunt Bessie. You have no idea how much I have needed someone here," she pressed. "I'm almost afraid to leave Aunt Bessie even with Irma."

That revelation called for a hurried explanation, so hurried that the buzzer was buzzing and Bobbie was at the door before the girls could "get their faces straight," as Cecy whispered to Sylvia.

"Hello, Bobbie!"

But Bobbie seemed thunderstruck. He just stood a moment gaping at Sylvia until Cecy had to repeat her greeting.

"Oh, hello, Ceece." He finally managed to overcome his amazement at Sylvia's good looks, and then accepted the introduction.

Sylvia was shy, that was obvious, and between them Cecy had her hands full getting things started.

"We can't go far, Bobbie," she began. "Sylvia's been traveling all day and Aunt Bessie needs me——"

"Come along," he agreed, his nice fishhook curls resisting the push back he gave them on his moist forehead, and his general appearance showing how carefully he could fix up for a ride with the girls.

Cecy gave very definite instructions to Irma, especially about not opening the inside door to strangers, and she was glad to note how efficient Irma seemed to be, and how intelligently responsive she was to Cecy's orders.

Already Bobbie was towing Sylvia along; easy to see he was captivated by this little beauty. But Cecy didn't mind, in fact she was glad of it. Maybe Bobbie would be able to help out nicely.

They were just ready to step in Bobbie's car that waited at the turn, in the lovely shrub-edged drive at the front of the handsome apartment, when Sylvia exclaimed.

"Oh, see that poor little dog over there under the bushes; he's hurt," and before Bobbie or Cecy could tell where the dog was, Sylvia skipped over the low hedge and was dashing down through the prim landscaped front grounds, while the doorman, who had been standing beside the car, showed signs of having a fit.

"The gardens!" he cried, clapping his gloved hands, "She mustn't spoil them."

"Gosh!" said Bobbie in his uncertain voice. "I could have gone after it."

"Not when Sylvia saw it first," Cecy told him, and in that moment she was remembering a little girl in Melody Lane who used to climb trees and rescue things, as well as rescuing sick babies she might have found in perilous situations.

Bobbie started off to meet Sylvia as she was coming back with a small black dog in her arms.

"Poor little thing," she was saying. "I'm afraid his leg is broken."

Cecy went closer. "Why—he's our Snippy!" she cried. "Snippy!"

Leg broken or not, Snippy fought desperately to get away from Sylvia and to Cecy. He barked and cried, and gave out those queer little yelps with which dogs try to express their feelings when something happens, like seeing Cecy again, something they just can't stand, they're so tickled to death about.

"Your dog!" Sylvia asked for now she had handed him over to Cecy.

"Yes." Cecy was looking at something fastened to Snippy's collar. It was a note, and her face became very serious as she saw even a few letters scrawled on the outside. She put her hand over it to hide it from Sylvia.

The queer letters were written by a foreign hand, that was perfectly plain, probably by—an Egyptian!

"Your own dog!" said Bobbie, wondering without knowing a thing about it all.

"Yes; we left him out in Rumson with Peter, he's Aunt Bessie's chauffeur," said Cecy holding poor little Snippy very gently so as not to hurt the injured leg. "Sorry to spoil the ride, Bobbie," she said next, "but I must see what I can do for him."

CHAPTER XV

POOR LITTLE SNOB

IT WAS more than a week later when Cecy again tried to show Sylvia that Aunt Bessie needed her help, as well as she needed Cecy's own.

That afternoon when poor little Snippy came crawling back to his mistress and to Cecy, crawling as far as he could go, then falling under the sheltering bush to be rescued by the impulsive Sylvia, he brought along with him a new threat.

It was in that note that Cecy had found tied to his collar. Quickly taking him into the tradesmen's entrance of the apartment while Sylvia begged her to let her, Sylvia, attend to him because "she knew a lot about dogs," Cecy had deciphered the message or threat. It read:

"Here is your dog. We come later."

There was no pretense of signature, but those foreign letters were certainly made either by Malika or by one of her tribe.

The coming of Sylvia had made a difference with Cecy; she could now talk to Sylvia and so save Aunt Bessie from discussing troublesome details, and on the other hand, Aunt Bessie felt free to keep things from Cecy. "Those girls shouldn't be dragged down with threats and alarms," she had decided. "I have people to protect us here."

So Cecy and Sylvia had not shown to Aunt Bessie the note Snippy brought; they merely told her they had found the dog trying to find her. She was glad to see him, and had the man in the basement take care of him and have a doctor attend to his leg, but Peter, out in the country, had been very much excited over the dog's escape from his place. He declared over the phone, he had seen a strange dark man sneaking around just before Snippy had disappeared, and that he had notified the police.

There had been a lot of excitement that afternoon and evening. Even Bobbie Ellis, who did finally manage to give the girls a ride, seemed surprised that a little black dog could "cause all that row." But Bobbie knew nothing of the note under Snippy's collar, nor the threat it carried.

"Miracles will never cease," declared Aunt Bessie to Cecy when they were alone, that very evening. "As long as I live I shall never forget how I felt when I went out and left you and Sylvia to fight it out. And when I came back and found you practically in each other's arms—Well, no wonder I went to bed and fell sound asleep. I needed pleasant dreams to wind up that day, if ever I needed them."

"I was almost as surprised as you were," Cecy admitted in answering. "Poor Sylvia was almost in hysterics and I didn't know what to do with her."

"But you found out," Aunt Bessie had answered shrewdly. "You youngsters do seem to stumble upon answers that we oldsters can't even figure out."

It was then that Cecy confessed. Bobbie Ellis had called with the boy he had been so anxious to have meet Sylvia, but the new boy had brought along another girl. Bobbie had fixed that up so he, himself, might be with Sylvia, as Cecy had declared she just couldn't go out that evening.

So while that little party was at the movies, Aunt Bessie and Cecy had an opportunity to have a good talk.

Cecy felt she should tell Aunt Bessie what she thought about Sylvia's predicament. But to do that she would have to clear up her own secret and frankly admit that she used to live in Melody Lane. She did that too.

"You see, Aunt Bessie," she had begun, "I was so crazy to get the work perhaps I couldn't think straight on anything else, and when you took it for granted that I had been in the Midwest a long time, I never thought of such a thing as going into the past and Melody Lane," she declared frankly.

"I understand perfectly," Aunt Bessie had assured her, "and I hate to think where I would be now, without you, if once again a young girl had not stumbled in where an old lady would have been afraid to tread."

"I feel so much better to have explained," Cecy went on. "Now I can tell you what I think about Sylvia."

"She seems all right now and quite happy," Aunt Bessie put in.

"Well, I'm afraid she isn't—neither all right nor happy. That's what I want to talk to you about. I knew this girl when she was a very strange child; a child that did things other girls would be afraid to attempt," said Cecy, "and I'm sure that's why she actually undertook to make herself over."

"Wasn't that the silliest thing?"

"And Miss Grant never meant her to do that, did she, Aunt Bessie?"

"Certainly not, it was all the girl's own doings. But when Nora heard what she was trying to do, of course, she wanted to praise her, not to blame her for it."

"And the poor little thing has just suffered agony. Do you suppose we could soon get in touch with Miss Grant, explain it all and have her write to you, telling Sylvia—I mean, doing something about it that would make Sylvia feel like herself again?"

"Nora's going to call me on Long Distance—" Aunt Bessie replied.

"But you could never explain all that on Long

Distance," Cecy interrupted. "I'll tell you. We'll fix up something with Bobbie that will take up a good part of an afternoon just as soon as we can. Then you and I will go over it all—you see *I* know all about Melody Lane—and, if you think best, I'll write it as clearly as we can in a letter to Miss Grant. Do you think that would do?"

"Yes, I do. I always find I can stick to things on paper that I flounder all over in, when I try to talk about them. We'll get together on that letter," Aunt Bessie decided.

"The meanest thing about all Sylvia's unhappiness," Cecy interposed "was the girls calling her a snob. It seems, when she would go off by herself the girls at school blamed her for being snobbish, when she was really too shy to mix with them. She told me she asked to have a little table by a window in the refectory after a sick girl left it, because she just felt she had no table manners and could not bear to eat when the girls were watching her. They called her a snob for that, of course," Cecy finished.

"Poor child," commented Aunt Bessie. "It seems as if all Nora's good intentions have failed to make her happy."

"But it isn't too late," Cecy insisted. "She's a sweet, adorable girl, and I haven't had any trouble since I talked to her that first day. I'll admit, I was sort of worried then, though."

"I expected to see you at each others' hair," joked Aunt Bessie, "and when I came back you were all serene. But how remarkable that you should have known this girl out in Melody Lane."

"Oh, no, it isn't really," answered Cecy. "You see, Melody Lane is a small place and we lived there a long time. Then my sister, Carol, always took part in the young girls' school social work and when they discovered need they helped the people. Or if they found trouble among poor people, as in the case of this girl's family, they jumped right in to help straighten things out. You have no idea what an interesting story this one of Sylvia's made."

"Oh, I heard snatches of it," Aunt Bessie replied. But she really could not have known the story of the Wild Warning to which Cecy referred. It was this story that related those remarkable adventures of Sylvia's earlier life, and which made one of the most interesting books of the Melody Lane series.

In all these confidential talks Cecy had never once mentioned the name of that little girl of Melody Lane who was now the disguised Sylvia. It seemed to her that Sylvia herself should be the first one to recall that almost famous name, that only a few years before had set everybody in the pretty little place ringing with the remarkable story of which she had been the heroine.

"I feel a lot better since I made my confession,"

Cecy now said a little shyly to Aunt Bessie. "I couldn't bear to feel I had been deceiving you about living out there."

"I forgive you, child," declared the lady sitting comfortably in the big chair in that big living-room. While the rooms were not actually so large, their arrangements and clever little decorative tricks gave that impression. As a matter of fact," said Aunt Bessie, her eyes twinkling until they cracked around the edges, "I purposely prevented you getting that explanation in. I wanted you and was taking no chances."

It was then that Cecy thought:

"But I haven't told her about the note on Snippy's collar. I'm going to, right now. No more deception for me, no matter what happens."

So she told her then and there.

"I thought this calm was too good to be true," Aunt Bessie replied, after Cecy had told her all about the note, even offering to show it to her, which Aunt Bessie decided there was no need for. She knew who had sent it, and she knew that they would keep their word. They would, as they said, "Come soon" for the mysterious Indian shawl.

"Don't you think you just ought to give it up, Aunt Bessie," Cecy proposed, uncertainly.

"That's the last thing I intend to do. It's mine; I paid for it, and if it's worth so much to them——"

"Oh, of course. I see what you mean. There

must be some strange mysterious value attached to it. A mere shawl, even if there is not another one in the world like it, could hardly cause all this secret intrigue," Cecy concluded.

"The trouble is we have Sylvia to straighten out at the same time, and we have got to be on guard every minute against these Egyptians," sighed Aunt Bessie. "When Peter phoned the other night after he missed Snippy, he said Malika had completely disappeared. I knew she would try to follow me, but I did feel safe here," she half sighed.

"And so we are safe," insisted Cecy. "You just wait and see what *two* girls, instead of one, can do about this. And the girl from Melody Lane, Sylvia to us now, can't have lost all her courage, even if they have been calling her a snob."

CHAPTER XVI

ANOTHER THREAT

WHEN Sylvia came in from her ride with Bobbie and his friends, her cheeks were tinted a good natural rose color and her hazel eyes were full of glints.

Cecy felt like teasing her, but remembering how shy she had been about going, she just said "I'll bet you had a swell time, you look it."

Sylvia made some funny but appropriate faces and skipped into her room with so much good nature and girlish cheer, that Cecy made a few appropriate faces herself; but Sylvia didn't see them.

Besides all this byplay there were arm pinches and secret nudges, and other highsigns such as lively girls pass around when they feel particularly happy.

"Let's go down and take Snippy for his run," Sylvia offered. "Come along, Cecy. You have been in all afternoon and it was wonderful out there on the Jersey Hills. You should have been along."

"Oh, I had a lot to do but I'll take a walk with you now," agreed Cecy. "This apartment is so different from the country place, I might get fat if

I don't get out more. Want anything, Aunt Bessie?"

"Yes, something from the drugstore," and she told her what, at the same time passing over the change and some extra for sodas if they weren't afraid those sweets would make them fat.

Sylvia raced ahead to get Snippy from his basement lodgings, and when the lively little fellow dashed out to Cecy he just couldn't make enough fuss over her. His injured leg was all right again, and when Sylvia snapped on his long leash they all trotted off, as if they hadn't a care in the world.

But after a few explosive sentences Sylvia suddenly fell silent. Noticing it Cecy asked her what was the matter.

"Oh, nothing," she replied evasively.

"But why so silent?"

"Just thinking."

"Could I know about what?" Cecy asked cautiously.

"Of course, Cecy. Only it seems sort of silly."

"Nothing interesting is silly, is it?"

Sylvia dropped Snippy's leash and let him have a run in his favorite lot by the pretty little stone church. She could watch him there and he wouldn't go beyond the ivied wall.

"Something happen this afternoon, Syl?" Cecy pressed affectionately.

"Well, nothing really happened," Sylvia replied. "But Bobbie is going back to school next week. He says he has to cram for some special exams."

"Oh, that's too bad, just when we began to have a good time. But then, don't worry. When we go in to see Carol, which I hope we will soon, she'll probably have a couple more vacation boys for us to show the town to. You see, her friend Ken has a lot of friends and they have small brothers."

"But I do think Bobbie is awfully nice," said Sylvia a little shyly.

"Yes, he is." It dawned upon Cecy that perhaps this new friendship of Sylvia's had meant more to her than it might have meant to herself, for instance. Having been so lonely, and so friendless, everything was ready for just such a change. And that, Cecy knew, would do Sylvia a lot of good.

"He made me think of our boys—" Sylvia stopped suddenly. She never seemed free to talk about Melody Lane. That was where she had lived among girls and boys she grew up with, and loved as if they had been her own brothers and sisters. And feeling she was obliged to give up all those memories to "be somebody else," had been the great mistake of her young life.

Cecy quickly filled up the gap in their conversation.

"Sylvia dear," she said gently, "Aunt Bessie has

been talking to me about all that, and she said Miss Grant merely agreed with you about all those changes. She had no idea of expecting you to make them, though. And you just wait. That's all going to be straightened out sooner than soon."

"But I will miss Bobbie," Sylvia persisted shyly.

"Yes, I know. I guess I will too. He is such a frank, free regular boy, isn't he?" Cecy felt obliged to assert her own interest at this point. "But as I told you, my sister Carol will be sure to have others just as jolly. But look, Syl, that man over there is whistling at Snippy."

They stopped to see a man just turning in from the sidewalk to the lawn at the side of the church, where Snippy was scampering about.

Sylvia's whistle, however, rang out clear and loud and little Snippy raced to the girls. Sylvia picked him up.

"Let's go home," said Cecy, her voice showing anxiety. "Look, he's coming toward us."

The man had turned quickly and was near enough to speak to the girls.

"That's the little black dog that carries letters, so?" he asked. He was, of course, a foreigner, well dressed and not bad looking.

"Come on," said Cecy to Sylvia, without noticing the stranger.

"Oh, you need not run, I won't hurt you," he

called as they were hurrying off. "But this time you, not the little dog, take message. Tell that lady we wait no longer. She will know."

Cecy was frightened. Sylvia had not yet heard about the Indian shawl mystery, so she asked what he could mean.

"Wait till we get home," whispered Cecy. "He's gone the other way," she could see as she half turned around. "Oh, Sylvia, now we must help Aunt Bessie, and forget our own silly selves for a while. I'm afraid she is in real danger."

They hurried back to the apartment, and quickly as she could, Sylvia put the little dog back in his pen in the basement and hurried to their own rooms with Cecy.

"I'm always afraid of really frightening Aunt Bessie," Cecy said in the corridor, "although she never shows the slightest fear. But now it does look dangerous. First, a note in Snippy's collar; I haven't had a chance to tell you about that, Sylvia," she hurriedly explained. "And now a man actually following us to threaten again."

They found Aunt Bessie waiting in her own room, but she came out at once, and at Cecy's earnest request sat right down with them in the living room to hear the latest report.

"But, Aunt Bessie," Cecy urged, "we must tell Sylvia. You know we had that all planned for this

evening but now we must hurry. There's no time
to lose."

"You can make better time than I can, Cecy,"
Aunt Bessie insisted. It was then that Cecy, in that
crisp exciting way of hers, started right in and told
Sylvia the story of the Indian shawl.

Of course, she could not go into all the interesting
details Aunt Bessie had given her, but the fact that
the shawl of a martyred Indian princess was at the
moment hidden in a simple bag in Cecy's closet,
right there within reach of them all, and that men
and women all the way from the desert had traced it
there and were determined to get it! Well! Just
as Cecy had said, that was enough and more than
enough to make both Cecy and Sylvia forget their
petty troubles, even forget that Bobbie Ellis and
his nice sports car wouldn't be coming around any
more, and even that a girl called Sylvia had been
living in strange dreams for months past. This was
no dream, no pretense, no young girl's idle romanc-
ing. It was a serious threat to the safety of all who
were associated with the mysterious Indian shawl.

"But they could never get in here," was Sylvia's
first conclusion, when Cecy had finished at least the
important points of the story. "This place is so
high up and all barred——"

"That's one reason why we came up here," sighed
Aunt Bessie. "But it seems an airplane in the clouds

would be no hindrance to those Egyptians. They'd go up higher and simply drop down on us."

"Would you feel better if we had a special watchman," Cecy proposed. "We could get one privately, you know."

"I'd rather not, not just yet anyhow," Aunt Bessie answered. "In fact, if they want to get in here, and of course they do, they're clever enough to outwit any watchman. I'll just try one more scheme, and if that doesn't work—Well, then perhaps I'll give them the shawl."

"After all you have gone through to save it," protested Cecy, "that would be awful."

"Why couldn't *I* just take the bag and go off some place with it," spoke up Sylvia. "Then, let them come in here and search for it. I wouldn't be afraid to do that. I could go—" She stopped, but Cecy knew she was just about to say she could go back to her own friends in Melody Lane.

"Dear child," said Aunt Bessie, solemnly. "I would no more let any one attempt to take that shawl either in a bag or hidden in any way, out of this place, than I would deliberately risk their lives. There's something about that bit of Kashmir that seems to attract those who are looking for it. No, my dears, I carried that shawl from the desert and it has pestered me every moment since. So, as I just said, unless a plan I am thinking of works out soon, I'll give them the nuisance and good riddance."

CHAPTER XVII

SOMETIMES CALLED FLINDERS

AUNT Bessie finally consented to ask the night hall man in the apartment to "look after this suite every hour or two as the girls were a little timid." They had all decided upon that excuse as being the most reasonable, although the girls were not really timid but simply being cautious.

"These apartments are so sound proof and so sort of isolated in spite of all being piled up on top of one another," Cecy had argued, "that nobody could hear if we did call."

"But you have the call button," Aunt Bessie reminded her.

"Yes, I know. But how could we get to the button if someone else got there first?"

So the hall man had been notified by Mr. Scott, the superintendent, and not only did he promise to "keep an eye on their quarters," but he threatened, Mr. Doyle was his name, "to make it hot for anyone who tried to sneak around *his* halls, day or night."

They liked Mr. Doyle, and felt better from his

assurance, and after a long evening of talking about the shawl and Aunt Bessie's experiences with it, they finally got to bed.

During the night Cecy heard someone moving around very cautiously. She lay so still listening, she scarcely breathed.

"Why didn't we have Snippy up with us," she was thinking. "I'm sure Mr. Scott would have made an exception for a few nights."

Then she heard a very light step approach her door. She instinctively put one hand to her throat, as she switched on her light with the other. Then she saw:

"Sylvia!"

"Did I scare you?" Sylvia whispered.

"Did you? Out of my very life. What's the matter? Get in here with me," Cecy invited, shifting her pillows to make room in her bed.

Sylvia looked sort of funny in the cheap cotton pajamas she had bought that first day, for their stripes looked like a ball-game, Cecy thought. But she was pretty, always pretty even in prison stripes. She got in with Cecy.

"Better put the light out," she suggested.

"All right," agreed Cecy, snapping it off. "What's the matter? Were you nervous?"

"No, not exactly, Cecy," Sylvia answered. "But after hearing all that story tonight about the shawl and how you and Aunt Bessie have been fighting to

save it, I just felt I would have to—well, tell you.
Of course you know I am Polly Cobb from Melody
Lane."

At last the old name was out, the admission was
made, and the girl known as Sylvia was again little
Polly Cobb, sometimes called Flinders.

Quickly, so that there might be no suspicion of
surprise about it, Cecy said:

"Certainly, who else would you be?   Nothing
surprising about that."

"Don't you think so, when I have never even
mentioned that name?   When I had tried to forget
it and when everyone called me a—snob?"

"Don't be silly," whispered Cecy.   "The girls
that started that were just jealous."

"But I did act snobbish.   How could they know I
was just scared—stiff?"

"Listen, Polly.   Do you like me to call you
Polly?"

For answer the girl threw her arms around her
companion and there was no other need for reply.

"But we'll wake Aunt Bessie, if we're not careful," Cecy continued.   "Here's what you and I have
got to do.   First, forget ourselves and our own
little troubles.   After all, we have made them for
ourselves.   I, for instance, planned doing so
much—"   She stopped short.   She did not want
Polly to offer her money and that's exactly what this
was leading up to.   "I mean," she whispered in that

waiting ear, "girls always have so many little things on their minds they just might neglect the real big things."

"To work out this shawl mystery? How could we?"

"We couldn't, of course. But first, suppose we tell Aunt Bessie in the morning that you would like to go back to your old name, Polly. She'll understand without asking a single question."

"Think so?"

"I know it," then Cecy whispered even lower, "she has already written that to Miss Grant."

Silence followed that important bit of information, but Cecy could guess that the girl who had been trying to be someone else, who had taken a strange name and was so wretched in her attempt at disguise, was actually giving in to a great sigh of relief.

"You know, I'm going to try to get Aunt Bessie to put the old shawl in the bank," Cecy ventured. "She rented a big box that day she had papers to sign, remember?"

"Oh, yes, the day I came. I wonder she didn't do that before," came Polly's question.

"You can be sure she had a good reason, whatever it may be," declared Cecy loyally.

"But about me. Is Aunt Bessie sure Nora would think it all right for me to—well, to give up what I was trying to do?" the girl asked hesitantly.

"Certainly she is. You see, Aunt Bessie must have talked several times on the phone with Nora, because she told me things Nora had said and I know there had been no time for letters."

"I suppose so," sighed Polly. "Of course Sylvia is a lovely name," she said next, "but I never felt right about it. It was too fancy for me. Imagine, after being Polly Cobb."

Cecy only made little sounds, but she was thinking:

"Imagine after being called Flinders, the heroine of the Wild Warning mystery." And this was really a sequel to that adventure.

"If only I could do some big thing for Nora," sighed Polly. "She has done so much for me and for Aunt Kate and the family. You know, I lived with Aunt Kate. She wasn't my real aunt," Polly went on, "but——"

"Oh, yes. I know," Cecy helped her out. "I heard that the Cobb girls and boys were at school now, and that your Aunt Kate has a nice position out in Melody Lane, housekeeper, isn't it? And she can go to her own home at night."

"Yes. It's lovely for them all. But I know they feel they should not have *lost* me to get it. Aunt Kate told me that."

"They haven't lost you. You'll see. You'll be going back there to visit them or even to live with them, if you want to," Cecy assured her. "Just wait a little while and *that* will be all straightened out. But our shawl mystery isn't so simple. It gets worse and worse."

At that very instant a light flashed in the window!

Polly sat up listening, ready to jump or give an alarm. Cecy noticed she showed not the slightest fear. Cecy also straightened up. Neither spoke. The light came again, it was diffused, as if sent in from a distance.

Without even whispering Polly slipped out of the bed and crept up to the window. The dim light from the transom over the door into the hall gave a little glimmer into the room, and now Polly was just lifting her head to the window sill to peer out.

"Yes," she whispered, "it's coming across the court from that building over there."

Cecy was beside her now. They were both hunched beneath the sill.

"It came from there once before, the very night we got here," she whispered. "Yes, see that small window on the second floor at the turn? There's someone standing there—see? They're directing a strong flash right over here. Oh!"

At that moment a flash of light was aimed straight at the girls' heads and they ducked quickly. After a few seconds Polly very carefully raised her head again and then Cecy followed.

"See," Cecy whispered, "there it is. And that's

a woman; I can see her sleeves. See, she's moving back——"

"Yes, it is a woman," said Polly. "And who's afraid of a woman."

They continued to watch. At that distance, Cecy was thinking, who's afraid of anyone, man or woman?

"You know," said Polly "this is fun, just like it used to be."

"But maybe if you had these scares as long as I have had them," Cecy reminded her, "they wouldn't seem funny. I'm glad, though, they aimed at my window instead of at Aunt Bessie's."

"And we can't call the hall watchman, Mr. Doyle, just because some one aims a light at us, I suppose," grumbled Polly.

"No, we can't and my foot's asleep. Let's get back to bed. See, the window's dark now. She's gone."

"Maybe coming over here——"

"Oh, Polly, don't" begged Cecy. "What's the use of looking for trouble?"

"Well," drawled Polly, who evidently was enjoying the small adventure, "if you look for trouble and find it you see it first, and can get after it. Don't you think so?"

Cecy didn't argue the point, and they crept back into bed. She, of course, was thinking of all the threats, of those men following Aunt Bessie out in the country and now here, and of Malika. Somehow thinking of Malika made Cecy shiver, or was the other window open too much?

"Come on in my room," begged Polly. "There are those two lovely beds—Oh, dear," she sighed suddenly, "I wonder why Nora thought I should have such grand things? Me, little Polly Cobb."

"Why not?" quickly answered Cecy, "You see, these apartments are made up in the grand manner to suit most people who can afford them, and Aunt Bessie just happened to spy this one, away up high and she liked it. Peek out and see if there's any more light."

"Nope; black as coal. Come on. Don't let's wake Aunt Bessie."

Cecy had made up her mind to speak to Mr. Doyle about the apartment where the light had come from, so when she got a good chance to get out early, before the day-man came on duty she slipped out, leaving Polly sleeping soundly. She found Mr. Doyle almost asleep himself in his funny arm chair down by the fire escape.

He was on his feet instantly:

"Anything wrong, Miss?" he asked touching his cap.

"Oh, no. I just wanted to ask you if you know any of the tenants in that big red brick place just back of here?"

"Know them? Well, yes. I know the man in charge there, Steve Nelson, a nice fellow he is."

"Well, someone flashed a light from there into our window," Cecy told him. "If you step over here to this window I think I can point it out."

"That's about the store room, I think," Mr. Doyle told her. "But I'll get around there and Steve will soon find out. Glad you told me, Miss——"

"Duncan," supplied Cecy.

"Of course, Miss Duncan," Mr. Doyle went on. "Say nothing about it, please. There's nothing worse in an apartment than a scare," he whispered. "Seems like folks who live in these big places haven't enough to do, the women, I mean. They grab at anything for a bit of excitement. I'll see Steve first thing. And I'll bet whoever is flashing that light won't try it again," he concluded, as Cecy thanked him and tiptoed off.

But they didn't have to wait for Dan Doyle's investigation. Their buzzer sounded before they were ready for breakfast, and when Irma came back from answering it, she announced there was a lady in the foyer who wished to see Miss Duncan.

CHAPTER XVIII

MALIKA PLEADS

PERHAPS it was because of the night's disturbance, but at any rate Cecy again had those creepy shivers when she went out toward the door to see who wanted her. A woman was sitting on the little waiting bench, her head slightly turned toward the door. As Cecy approached she raised her head and looked at her.

"Malika!" exclaimed Cecy, under her breath.

"Hush!" whispered the woman, putting a finger to her lips. Then she motioned questioningly toward the open door of the reception room.

Nodding, Cecy walked in ahead of her. How different she looked, as if in some sort of uniform. Her long blue coat fitting her snugly, by no means seemed like anything that Malika had ever worn out in the country. And on her carefully arranged black hair was a small prim hat. Her hands were encased in light gloves and she was carrying quite a large sized, good leather handbag. Could this really be Malika?

146

But it was. Those sharp black eyes still flashed their hidden fires, and Malika was sitting so close to Cecy on the divan, the girl felt smothered beneath her.

"I must talk so fast," Malika began. "I have only a little time. They might find I came here. Last night I flashed the light——"

"Oh, I saw it," murmured Cecy.

"Yes, I saw you and I know this is the right place——"

"But wait, Malika, I must call Miss Benedict," Cecy said, starting up.

"That you must not," and a hand drew her down again. "I can hardly talk so fast but I must. I came to beg you on my knees to give back the shawl. My poor old father is in prison. They put him there, they beat him, they starve him, because he lost that shawl." The woman's expression changed to a look of real pleading and entreaty and she seemed about to seize Cecy's hands, but Cecy avoided that.

"It is not my father who is the thief; no, old Mohammed is an honest man, a holy man," declared the woman. "But those thieves bring this priceless shawl to his place to hide it. He did not know that. They put it in with his own shawls on his back shelf and then—it is gone."

Cecy remembered that was exactly what Aunt Bessie had said; that was how the old man had handed this shawl to her, wrapped in another Kashmir.

"When it is gone they go for him, they beat him, and I, his daughter Malika, go out quickly from the desert and follow this lady when she goes for boat. The other men say 'all right,' if I can get it they let my father go.

"But I can't ever get it. No, please," Cecy was again moving as if to call Aunt Bessie, "I must go back before they find me," said Malika. "They now give me three more days. They are come to New York City. Men follow you everywhere." She made wide motions with her hands. "But, please, oh, please, Miss, Cecy, as you love your own father, you do this for me. Or my father he will sure die." The woman covered her face with her hands as if to shut away that sight.

"Here, take this ring," she was slipping a big ring with that rough stone Cecy had noticed before, over to Cecy now. "This is our sign. When you send me this I will come. Do not give to anyone but Malika. I must go. They find me—Here is where to write me." She put a small card into Cecy's hand. She was breathless and so was Cecy.

And it was then that this Malika, who seemed so different from that country woman, even talking now in that queer broken English, again fell into a familiar figure.

She left the room so noiselessly and opened and

shut that heavy door so quickly, Cecy had scarcely
time to see her going.

But she was gone.

Stunned, Cecy sat there. She was holding the big
antique ring, but now she let it drop into her lap
like something sinister; as if the carved beetle on the
ring now emiting those opalescent lights peculiar
to the scarabs of Egypt, would fly at her, sting her,
even poison her. But it was only a stone, a bluish
green beetle and Cecy had not yet seen the hiero-
glyphics carved beneath. But they were carved
there, those queer characters the ancients used to
depict words.

"Cecy!"

Both Aunt Bessie and Polly had spoken at once.

"What is the matter?" exclaimed Aunt Bessie.

"Whoever was that?" demanded Polly.

"Oh, the child's ill," Aunt Bessie began again.

"No, I'm not really," said Cecy finally. "It's
just that—I'm sort of stunned——"

"Who was that? What's that ring?" Aunt
Bessie was just going to pick the ring up from Cecy's
lap when Cecy put her hand to it.

"Wait," she said, a little shakily. "Let's go inside. Then I'll tell you."

"But you'll have your coffee before you fall
apart," Polly insisted. "If you haven't had a ghost
caller this early morning—" She stopped. No
time for jokes now. Cecy's face was proof enough

that the caller must have been a ghost or even worse.

"Land sakes," began Aunt Bessie. "I wondered what was keeping you. But I was giving Irma some orders. They might have carried you away. Let me see that ring."

"It's Malika's——"

"I know it. She wore that always," declared Aunt Bessie. "Let's wash it there at the basin. I never like to touch their things——" She had picked the ring up from Cecy's hand very gingerly, and was now beside the bathroom basin letting the hot water run on it. Back again into her bedroom where they had all gone for privacy, Aunt Bessie was scrutinizing the ring.

"Irma is calling for breakfast," Polly told them "and see how late it is. Let's go talk in the dining room."

So they went in there, and although Irma moved around like the "perfect peach" that they all so often declared her to be, there was no need for them to fear her listening. Whatever she heard she had never showed the slightest interest in.

"Malika came to beg us to save her father," Cecy started. "He's the man you bought the shawl from, Aunt Bessie."

"Save him, how?" Polly asked first.

"She says they have him in prison, that they beat

and starve him, and oh, Aunt Bessie, if you ever saw the agony in Malika's face you would believe her," said Cecy solemnly.

"Maybe I would. But what can I do?" Aunt Bessie asked in real bewilderment.

"I suppose give her back the shawl——"

"Oh, no, please don't do that," interrupted Polly. "You bought it for Nora, didn't you, Aunt Bessie? And can't we give it to her? Wouldn't it be wonderful for Nora to have the shawl of an Indian Princess?"

Instantly the same thought flashed into the minds of both Aunt Bessie and Cecy.

Little Make-believe! She would care more for that than for the suffering of an old man in the desert. Or couldn't she imagine that? Was the idea too strange to Polly for her to realize it?

"But if that old man is in prison, . . ." Cecy attempted.

"Maybe we could get him out," spoke up Polly. "Some people will do anything for money. Oh, I've just been thinking. If only Aunt Bessie would let *me* give the shawl to Nora, perhaps I could do—well—do something for you in return, Aunt Bessie," she faltered.

They fell silent for a moment. This interruption bothered Cecy. *She* had to think fast of Malika and her tragic message.

"She has only three days, you know, Aunt Bessie," Cecy went on, almost ignoring Polly's agitation. "We've got to do something quickly."

"Did you promise her?" Polly asked anxiously.

"I didn't have to. I'm sure she knew I believed her and pitied her," said Cecy slowly.

"Let me have that card," Aunt Bessie directed Cecy, referring to the card Malika had given her.

"Oh, I would never go to a strange place without your permission," Cecy said a little indignantly, handing over the cardboard piece.

"I know that, Cecy, but I'm responsible for you to your family and I must do my part too. I'll call my lawyer in New York tomorrow and tell him the whole story. I'm still convinced that those people would not make all this fuss over a mere shawl," Aunt Bessie finished rather dramatically.

"It doesn't seem as if they would," Cecy added. "And if you ever saw and heard Malika! Honestly, I felt as if *I* were in the desert being smothered with——"

"Sand," popped in Polly, who was not taking this matter as seriously as the others were. But then, it was new to her and she could not possibly know all the dangers it entailed.

"But how on earth did Malika ever get in here?" Aunt Bessie asked Cecy.

"You wouldn't know her. She was dressed in sort of blue uniform——Oh, I know," Cecy exclaimed suddenly. "I didn't think of that before. It was a uniform, the uniform of a visiting nurse and she was wearing it so she could get in easily."

"The uniform of a visiting nurse?" Aunt Bessie repeated. "Wherever would she get that?"

"Maybe borrowed it," Polly suggested.

The phone was ringing. Cecy sprang up to answer it. And it was Carol, her sister, who had been expecting Cecy and Polly and wondered why they couldn't run in to see her and their dad.

It took some evasive answers to satisfy Carol, but Cecy knew she could not leave the scene of excitement *that* day, and she finally made Carol understand that she was well, perfectly fine but busy with some little important tasks she didn't like to leave unfinished.

"But we *are* going in in a day or two. You just see if we don't. And tell Dad—Oh, no never mind, Sis, I'll tell him myself," Cecy finished, knowing that reply would be taken to mean that she surely would run down home soon. So Carol had to be satisfied.

Next the buzzer sounded and Cecy also went to attend to that. Opening the door she found the night watchman, Mr. Doyle standing there.

"Sorry to bother you, Miss," he began, "but early this morning I found a woman loitering about here. First, when she came up I thought she was a nurse and I let her pass. But when she came out—from your door it was—I thought she acted suspicious."

"There had been a woman here," Cecy quickly told him.

"I know, that's what I'm sayin', Miss. But when she came out and I spoke to her, she started to run, and I ran after her."

"Oh, that was a woman who used to work for us," said Cecy in alarm.

"Was it, now? Well, just to make sure, I took her down to the police station——"

"Malika is arrested?" Cecy almost moaned, seeing at once the great danger of such a move as that.

"Well, she's just being held. And if Miss Benedict knows her, I'll go with her myself and explain," offered Dan Doyle. "You can't be too careful, Miss, with them strangers around."

CHAPTER XIX

THE RUNAROUND

IT WAS surprising how much excitement could be whipped up in that apartment by three persons, each begging the other to take it easy and not get excited.

"But if those men ever find out Malika had been here, that she was arrested in our very own hall," Cecy was trying to point out, "there's no telling what they would do to her."

"Would they kill her, do you suppose?" Only Polly would ask that sensational question.

"Where's my fan? It's warm today. Thanks, Cecy. Yes, I'll put on that little hat. Did you call the cab? Be sure you stay right here, Polly. There must be some—of the family—on hand to answer the phone." Aunt Bessie said all that on a short wave breath and it almost did for her.

"Mr. Doyle is waiting down at the cab," said Cecy. "Dear me! I hope people won't see us going into the police station."

"No harm if they do. We might be going there to enter a protest against last night's band concert in the park. It was pretty noisy, it strikes me."

Aunt Bessie was always ready with an answer, and one that sounded all right, too.

They got into the cab, and Dan Doyle slipped into the front seat and was chatting away with the driver before Aunt Bessie had succeeded in drawing on her silk gloves, and before Cecy had straightened her belt. It was only a short run over to the group of buildings, the bank, the post office, and a very nice-looking matching building with its sign: Police Station.

Cecy felt a little fluttery because she alone realized what this might mean to Malika—if those men found her there or found out she was there. But Aunt Bessie quickly disposed of all unnecessary questions, assuring the man behind the shiny brass rail that this was her maid and she was no suspicious character.

Malika was white in spite of her natural dark color, and her eyes stood out like electric bulbs, Cecy thought. She certainly was frightened, Malika was, and never ventured a single word during the hurried proceedings. All she wanted to do was to get out of that place, and the others, including Dan Doyle, apologizing for his mistake, were anxious to help her do so.

There was plenty of room in Aunt Bessie's especially large cab, but Malika crammed herself far back in the corner and out of the window range.

She had been directed by Aunt Bessie to sit there rather than alone in the little folding half seat so conspicuously set out between.

"Let me see, where to?" pondered Aunt Bessie.

"If you just let me out any place, Miss Benedict, and I thank you very much," murmured Malika.

"No, not any place. First, we must talk, we must settle this. Tom," to the driver, "take us to that little dress shop you took me to the other day," Aunt Bessie ordered.

"The dress shop?" queried Cecy.

"Yes. There's a little room there where we can talk privately, and you can buy a dress later if you want to. A dress shop is about the—best place." She had been just going to say "the safest place," but she changed it.

A block further on Dan Doyle dropped out, smiling and happy as ever, even if he had given folks a "bit of trouble." In fact he seemed rather proud of himself.

At the dress shop a smiling and very neat young girl opened the door as the slivery bell tingled. Aunt Bessie greeted her familiarly, and said they were going in the little green room to talk about what they might want. The girl, Estelle it seemed was her name, ushered them into that little corner room, and after a moment or two Cecy very gently pushed the door closed.

Malika still acted frightened, as if it might be Aunt Bessie's turn to accuse her now.

"We must talk fast *this* time if ever," Aunt Bessie began. "Malika, I remember your father——"

"My poor old father," sighed the woman.

"And I believe your story, the one you told Cecy. You say these spies have warned you they would only wait three days longer?"

"Only three days," whispered Malika, despair fairly dripping from her deep-toned voice. "And that Sam he means it. He is a dreadful bad man."

"All right. Now here is what you must do. Can you go right back to New York?"

"New York, now?"

"Yes, on the next train," went on Aunt Bessie. "Have you people there you can stay with?"

"Oh, yes, plenty people in New York. My cousins——"

"Then, that's all right. Have you any money?"

"Money? Some."

"I'll give you some more." Cecy sat there not saying a word, but Aunt Bessie pushed on relentlessly.

"Now, Malika, I won't go over all the things I blamed you for. I supposed you were forced to try to scare me into giving *it* up."

"Yes, yes, Miss Benedict. I never want to do that. I came all the way from Cairo, follow you and do ever'ting to save my poor old father," whis-

pered Malika, unhappily.   Her big eyes were glazed
with tears.

"But *what* are they after?" demanded Aunt
Bessie. "Just that shawl?"

Malika opened her eyes wider.   She glanced
furtively at the window, then she shook her head.

"Maybe," she said.   "But they tell me now they
will get you for *smuggling* if you do not give up."

"Smuggling!" repeated Cecy.

"Indeed," Aunt Bessie answered, "I declared that
shawl and paid duty on it. Smuggling, indeed!"

"I don't know."   Malika seemed sorry she had
used the word, but somehow both Cecy and Aunt
Bessie seemed to feel it meant a lot more than the
woman was ready to admit.

"Well, here's my plan," the indomitable Aunt
Bessie continued. "Here's some more money." She
gave Malika a bill. "You go right to New York.
Pay your fare on the train so you won't have to go
in the station at all.   Then, if they're hanging around
there looking for you, they won't have a chance
even to get on the train, and I'll have Tom, our
driver, drive right up to the last car just in time for
you to step on."

"Oh, Aunt Bessie," urged Cecy, "you are getting
all excited. Please don't. Here's your fan," and in
handing the fan to the very much flushed lady, Cecy
tenderly patted her soft lace collar back into place.
It had sort of blown up into a choker.

"Yes, dear. I know——"

"But please, Miss Benedict, how will I get it? You are very careful of it, yes? You keep it wrapped up in box?"

"Of course, Malika. In fact, we haven't even looked at it——" Aunt Bessie stopped suddenly. Better not say anything about the shawl, not give even Malika an idea where it might possibly be kept.

Cecy's look at Aunt Bessie was knowing and understanding. She was thinking it was about time they did take a look at that shawl, but trailing that thought came the next: but this is not the time for us to tell anyone, even Malika that. It was in that box in Cecy's closet, the door locked and the key safe. Polly had asked Cecy why they couldn't take it out, but Cecy had simply said they couldn't.

"Oh!"

It was Cecy who had uttered the exclamation. A man had pushed open the door and stuck his head in. It was a very black head.

"Excuse me," he said most politely. "I did not know anyone was here," and he left taking his head, of course, with him.

"Whoever was that?" gasped Cecy.

"I don't know," said Aunt Bessie, "but we must find out. Go out, dear, and ask for Estelle. Tell her to come in here to see about our order."

"Can't I go now?" begged Malika. "I walk to train."

"Just a minute and we'll all go," Aunt Bessie promised.

Cecy was walking out in the little shop among the pale green and silver fitting booths, and the racks of lovely summer things. She saw Estelle who came up to her immediately.

"Can you see Miss Benedict now?" Cecy asked.

"Certainly," Estelle smiled back, and they hurried to the small green room in the corner.

"Oh, there you are," Aunt Bessie told them. "Estelle, we find we can't wait today but I want you to know Miss Duncan, Cecy," she added pleasantly. "She'll be in again in a day or two and I want you to take good care of her. Sorry, we must hurry— Oh, by the way—who was the man who poked his head in?" she asked casually.

"Oh, did he do that? Sorry. That was Victor, madam's brother. He was looking for a model. He thought he left it in here," said Estelle in apology. "Sorry he disturbed you."

"That was *one* false alarm," Cecy remarked as they were all in the cab again going toward the station.

"Wasn't it? Goes to show how jittery we are. Now, Malika, here is a New York address and a telephone number. Be there, let me see, today is Tuesday. Be there Thursday morning at ten o'clock and I'll call you, positively."

"But, please, Miss Benedict, will I then get the

shawl? You see, I can go back to Cairo when I know for sure—I mean, when I have it to take back with me," she corrected herself.

"Now, Malika, I've done all I can just now. You can depend upon me; I will not break my promise. And you need not worry about your father. I'll see that he is released from wherever he is being held."

"The ring, Aunt Bessie," Cecy said aside. "Don't you want to give that back to her now?"

"Oh yes, of course I do." Aunt Bessie looked in her handbag and soon produced the ring.

"You keep that. It is a guarantee," declared Malika. "I leave it for—good word."

"No, we don't need it. We don't really want it," Aunt Bessie answered, thinking how little she wanted anything that would connect her with the mystery. "You take it; better put it right on. It's a lovely ring. Now, there's the station. Tom!" she called to the driver, "if it's time for the train drive right over to that crossing."

Cecy was amazed at Aunt Bessie's efficiency. She was actually getting Malika on that train before she seemed to realize she was going any place. That was exactly what Aunt Bessie was determined to do, of course.

"But if I go—" Malika was trying to hold back.

"Help her up, Tom, it's a high step," Cecy undertook to order, for that rear step was high and there was no trainman there with the stepping stool.

"Oh, she's gone!" sighed Aunt Bessie in sheer relief, when Tom was back in his seat and the train had puffed away on the curve.

"That was quick work," Cecy said quietly. "Don't you think we had better drive back the other way? You know that road that runs around the park?"

"Yes, do that, Tom," Aunt Bessie ordered. "Let's get away from these publi streets. My, my!" she sighed. "I talked so fast I feel like a three way switch. Cecy, is my hat on or did I leave it in the dress shop?" That was the best part of Aunt Bessie. She never lost her sense of humor.

"I wonder what Polly has been doing all this time," Cecy reflected. They were passing the little stone church where the strange man had spoken to them a few days before.

"Do you know, I love to hear you call her Polly," Aunt Bessie said. "It seems to suit her. Sylvia is a lovely name but not for the child. I'm so glad you changed it."

"She is too," said Cecy. "But still, she's very anxious to hear from Miss Grant about it."

"I am too. If it were not for this other matter— Do you realize, Cecy," she interrupted herself "we have been running around after each other and even after ourselves for a full month? And that summer is going fast?"

"Yes, I do, Aunt Bessie. But don't you think we

did a good deal with all this running around, as you call it?"

The pleasant middle aged woman gave Cecy one of her choicest smiles.

Then Tom turned into their driveway.

CHAPTER XX

ONLY THREE DAYS MORE

POLLY was in the telephone corner when they entered the apartment.

"I'm just glued to this phone," she pouted. I don't dare leave it to get a drink of water. There was a long distance call and, of course, they wouldn't give it to me."

"For me?" Aunt Bessie asked, although she knew it must have been.

"Yes. The operator said in a high and mighty voice: 'Los Angeles calling. For Miss Elizabeth Benedict.' I said, in my sweetest voice, 'Miss Benedict isn't here but *I* can take the message,'" Polly went on, and the way she imitated the operator as well as her own "sweetest voice" was funny enough to excuse this long drawn out answer.

"But it seems *I* couldn't take the message. The Long-distance-calling just asked when did I expect her and said she would call then," Polly finished quite grumpily.

"They'll call. That was from Nora. I've been expecting it," said Aunt Bessie.

"Expecting what, Aunt Bessie?" Polly asked.

"Well, just a message telling me she agrees with everything," Aunt Bessie stumbled.

"You have told her about me?"

"Yes, of course I did. And she has already sent me a long night letter about it."

"What—what did Nora say?" Polly was very earnest now and again assumed that look of wonder that made her lovely hazel eyes glint golden sparks.

"She said, of course, she was happy to have you understand better. That there really could never have been another Sylvia, and that she herself had been very upset and entirely out of her natural self when she even thought of such a thing."

"Oh, I'm glad," said Polly simply.

"Now, listen Aunt Bessie," Cecy began firmly, "you've just got to lie down. You've been going like a house a-fire——"

"And I feel like one. All right, girl. I'll lay me down. Oh, I am so glad to get that woman away from here," she sighed, beginning to loosen up her things.

"And away from our windows," Cecy added. "Now it's our turn, Aunt Bessie, Polly and I have been wanting to do certain things, but we didn't like to interfere with you. But surely, after this morning, you are willing to give us a chance." Cecy had fixed the shade and given Aunt Bessie her favorite toilet water. She used a lot of it in hot weather.

"Go ahead. Do your worst. The sooner we jump right into things now the better," said Aunt Bessie. "Three days go by quickly."

"But what had you planned to do? What message are you going to give Malika Thursday morning?" Cecy was anxious to know.

"I intended to talk to my lawyer, make sure I was on safe ground and that if I gave up the shawl it would be to the right party," Aunt Bessie replied. "But I don't know about that now. You heard what Malika said about smuggling."

"Smuggling?" Polly grabbed that word eagerly.

"Yes. I think that was a slip of Malika's," Aunt Bessie told the girls. "It was plainly uppermost in her mind but she seemed sorry the moment she uttered the word."

"I noticed that, too," Cecy agreed. "But what would the old shawl have to do with smuggling? Oh, of course I see now. It must be very valuable and the duty you paid, Aunt Bessie, would be claimed an under value."

"Well, *I* didn't hide any value," Aunt Bessie insisted. "And that Arab gentleman I met on the boat from Alexandria could not have seen anything very unusual about the shawl or he would have told me so."

"You said he examined that paper that was pinned on it, remember?" Cecy reminded her. "Don't you know, he said that might be a real record of its age and that it actually had belonged to an Indian princess?"

"Oh, why can't we see it?" begged Polly. "There it is right in that closet."

"And here *we* are being watched all around, maybe," said Cecy in almost a whisper. "I'm dying to see it, too, but I wouldn't try to look at it now."

"No, not now," said Aunt Bessie. "We must *all* look at it and enjoy it and maybe find some nice old ghost hidden in it," she joked. "But when we do the doors will be double locked and all the curtains drawn."

"Tonight?" Polly asked. "Could we take it out tonight?" she coaxed.

"Better not plan any particular time," said Cecy, feeling very old womanish in trying to restrain Polly when she was just dying to see the mysterious Kashmir herself. Often at night she had imagined the thing either crawling through a crack in the door or sending some bejeweled desert snakelet to do the crawling. But Polly had to be kept under control. There was no telling what she might try to do if they did not check her. And since hearing the direct word from Nora Grant she seemed even gayer than ever. What a change from that moody taciturn girl that Cecy had first encountered.

Just when they had hoped to have a little rest, all three of them, after lunch which for Aunt Bessie was merely ice cream and cookies and a big drink of Irma's incomparable lemonade, taken right in her bed room on the bedside table, and just when Cecy had finally convinced Polly that a half hour of quiet might even do her good, the telephone rang.

Cecy hurried to catch it before it disturbed Aunt Bessie. It was Peter, out in Rumson, and he was not like Polly's Long Distance lady, *he* gave the message to Cecy.

He was telling her, to tell Miss Benedict of course, that there had been men around the house out there who claimed to want to buy the place. Since the place was for sale, although all Aunt Bessie's things were in it, Peter wanted to know what to do about it.

"Aunt Bessie likes the place, doesn't she, Peter?" Cecy asked, explaining first that Aunt Bessie was resting just then.

"She does, Miss," Peter answered, "and she said she might buy it herself if she got some woman friend to live out here with her."

"Then, I'll tell you, Peter," suggested Cecy as if she knew all about things she didn't know a thing about, "just tell the real estate man he will hear from Miss Benedict herself in a few days."

"That's fine," came back the voice over the wire, "for, as a matter of fact, I think they're the same set that came out here and sneaked Snippy away. They have those black eyes with a lot of white around them," Peter described, curiously.

Then he wanted to know how Snippy was, and Cecy hurried to get finished before her voice would reach the sleeping lady.

"So they are working on all fronts," she was thinking as she broke off the connection. "That old shawl must be worth its weight in gold to have all those men paid to get it back. Oh, how wonderful if it should turn out to be worth a fortune for Aunt Bessie!"

"More telephone calls?" Polly complained.

"Yes, that was Peter, our man out in the country, you know," Cecy said in a low voice. "And listen, Polly, I'm really frightened now. Peter says some strange men want to buy the house out there. Of course, they only want to search it, but they must know Aunt Bessie wouldn't leave the shawl out there."

"Maybe Malika told them that just to throw them off the track to get more time," suggested Polly.

"Oh, yes, that could be it. We did leave in an awful hurry and Malika didn't see us leave either," reasoned Cecy. "But somehow, Polly, I'm getting to feel it may be more dangerous than we have realized. You see, Aunt Bessie is so very determined and the more trouble they made to get the shawl the more she fought them. But suppose anything should happen to her? If she can't give

Malika satisfaction when the three days are up I feel sure they'll get in here somehow——"

"Oh, Cecy, you're just being nervous. And you aren't, usually, you know," Polly tried to tell her. "Aunt Bessie said she was going to call her lawyer in New York tomorrow, didn't she?"

"Yes, she did."

"Then perhaps he'll fix things up." That was just as vague as had been all their other ideas.

"But we must make Aunt Bessie rest," Cecy insisted. "Her face flushed so today. I was afraid she might get sick."

"She was going to let us see the shawl tonight," Polly reminded Cecy.

"But that can wait," persisted Cecy. "Much better to wait until Aunt Bessie is rested, don't you think so?"

"Why, why should that bother her? Of course, I don't want to be selfish," Polly hurried to add, "but I thought we might discover something about it if we ever had a chance to look it over."

"Yes, that's so. Well, if she rests now perhaps it will be all right," Cecy agreed. "But you know, Polly, it is sure to excite her. Just think how she carried it from the desert and how she has kept it hidden——"

"For Nora, Cecy. I do so hope it can be given to Nora, that I can give it to her," Polly murmured.

"I know it would be Aunt Bessie's gift, of course, but if she'd just let me send it or if Nora comes let me give it to her. I would feel I hadn't sort of backed out of everything."

"It's only a shawl," Cecy protested.

"Oh, I know. And Nora can get shawls from any part of the world. But with all this exciting story. Well, don't you think it might be a brand new kind of publicity for a famous actress?"

Cecy looked at the girl who seemed to be something of an actress herself, though not yet famous.

"I see what you mean, Polly," she replied, "and maybe it would be a new kind of publicity. But I'm afraid you've been reading a lot of movie magazines," she finished jokingly.

"Don't you like them?"

"If I did Aunt Isabel, with whom I've been living, you know, wouldn't. So I don't see them often," Cecy explained. "But, Polly, this horde of strange people following us around is getting pretty serious. I wish I were near enough my sister Carol to talk to her about it. She's had such a lot of experience."

"But then *we*, you and I, wouldn't be—" Polly paused. She didn't like to be vain enough to say that they could not get the glory of working the mystery out if they merely followed Carol's advice.

"Surely you don't believe in all that old fashioned

stuff about girls being detectives and heroes and such nonsense do you, Poll?"

"Oh, no, not the Pollyanna stuff. But then *we* might work it out and it would be wonderful if we did, wouldn't it?"

What was the use of trying to reason with a girl like Polly?

"Girls," called Aunt Bessie just then. "Did I hear the phone?"

"Yes, it was Peter," Cecy told her hurrying into her room to explain Peter's message.

"Well, I've made up my mind. I'll have that shawl all signed and sealed and certified by my lawyer tomorrow, or at the most the next day. Then on Thursday morning, as I promised, I'll turn it over to Malika. *I've* had enough of it."

CHAPTER XXI

LONG DISTANCE

THAT was Aunt Bessie's decision. As she announced it Polly's face fell to zero, Cecy thought, and she herself had to admit it was dreadfully disappointing.

After everything, just to give it up like that. Perhaps Aunt Bessie was all tired out. She seemed to be. But even Polly saw that she and Cecy were merely Aunt Bessie's guests, and had no right to interfere, especially now.

So the matter was suddenly dropped as if it were of no importance at all, when all three of them could think of nothing else. Polly had agreed with Cecy not to ask to see the shawl that evening, and the two girls went for a walk after dinner at Aunt Bessie's insistence, and decided to spend the rest of the evening writing letters. Irma was with Aunt Bessie while they were out, and getting back before dark, they were all ready to settle down when Aunt Bessie told Polly they would probably get that long distance call from Nora soon, as she would be likely to call only at certain times when she would be free to do so.

This made it impossible for Polly to even try to write her letter—that one to Aunt Kate out in Melody Lane and one other, important and very personal. She had so much news on such important matters for Aunt Kate's letter she couldn't even think of it until Nora had talked to Aunt Bessie and settled things. Cecy went off to her room and could hardly decide which letter to tackle first, her correspondence had gotten so far behind lately.

"I'm glad I did run down home those last few times," she was thinking as she got her letter things ready, "even if I did have to rush so. Of course, I couldn't wait to see Dad the last time and I missed him—" She stopped even her running thoughts then. Cecy and her Dad were great chums, and she began just lately to feel that it was hard on a girl to be away to school and away during vacation also.

But time was passing and soon this experiment would be over. Cecy Duncan had become genuinely fond of this Miss Benedict, who at first had seemed peculiar and even forbidding. But since understanding why she had acted that way, and appreciating the full trust Miss Benedict had given Cecy from the very first, the young girl now found herself completely in accord with Aunt Bessie.

"And that little Flinders flare-up," Cecy was recalling this evening. "What won't a romantic girl do when she is stuck with too much time on her hands?"

She would write to Rosie Wells first. Rosie would simply "blow up" when she came through New Jersey from the New York mountains and stopped off to see the Duncan family. Rosie always wrote and also answered Cecy's letters, but there had been a long gap on Cecy's side lately.

So she started bravely tonight. Polly must be reading instead of writing, Cecy suspected, and Aunt Bessie had been toying with a magazine a long time.

At last the phone jingled. Aunt Bessie picked up her bedside connection.

"Yes, this is Miss Benedict." She motioned to Polly to sit down, she had been standing in the doorway. After a moment Aunt Bessie said: "All right! Oh, is that you, Nora?"

Polly felt sort of breathless. Actually Nora Grant, who had done so much for her, was sending her voice over that long distance to talk about her, Polly Cobb. It seemed exciting when it came so close to reality.

"Oh, wonderfully, Nora dear," Aunt Bessie went on. "As happly as—" She paused listening to the other voice. "But there really was no mistake, dear. Don't feel that way. You just thought it was a grand idea and it was—" She stopped again and Polly noticed how serious she looked. "Yes, she's right here. Want to speak to her? Polly."

Polly stepped over to take the receiver. Her knees felt shaky. She who had jumped off roofs and climbed poles without a quake, now all but trembled as she picked up a telephone.

"Yes, Nora," she called back quite bravely. Then she was listening. Nora was saying:

"You did just what I wanted to do but I hadn't the courage. You are Polly again, and I like the little name—" She paused but Polly merely said "Yes," questioningly.

"After all, dear, my baby is gone. When it happened I had to do something. And you had risked your life to save her."

"But, Nora, you did so much, for all of us—" Polly had some courage now, but very little. She felt overwhelmed.

"But lately I've been afraid I had tried to do *too* much, to influence you I mean. But I must hurry a little," came the lovely velvet voice. "You understand, dear, you are to go right back to your own folks. I'll take care of things and I'll always— love—you!"

"But won't I see you again?" Polly had grasped at that threat. She idolized Nora Grant and could not let her go—now. She felt panic seizing her.

"Oh, of course. I'll be in New York this fall and

then we'll fix everything. Good-bye, darling, I know Aunt Bessie will do what's best. I must ring off now. Good-bye—darling—Polly!"

Carefully Polly placed the receiver in its cradle as if she hated to sever that connection. Nora Grant, who from the first had insisted upon being called Nora by Polly, had given her back to her Melody Lane family. She wouldn't have to go to boarding school now, she would not let anyone shampoo her hair and tell her there was nothing in the rinse to lighten it, she would manicure her own nails and use what Cecy used, and no one would ever again have a chance to call her a snob.

"Now wasn't that lovely, Polly? To speak to Nora all the way from the Coast?" Aunt Bessie was noticing Polly's puckered lips and wanted to change the subject quickly.

"Yes, lovely," was all Polly said. But she smiled happily through something like a little mist although not quite tears, as she slipped away to her own room. Aunt Bessie smiled too, but she did not try again to divert Polly.

"Poor child," she was thinking, "but it will be all right. In fact, it *is* all right. I'll make her run out to Melody Lane in a day or two and that's the real cure. Just to face things."

During the telephone interval Cecy had stayed in her room, but now she should see what Polly was doing. She found her with her suitcase spread out and her closet door wide opened.

"Oh, whatever are you doing?" Cecy asked in surprise.

"Well, I'm not running away, if *that's* what you thought," Polly answered brightly. "But you know, Ceece," she always said "Ceece" when she wanted to show her real affection, "I just wondered if you would help me get rid of some of these silly things?"

"Get rid of them? Why they're beautiful!"

"I know. But you can wear my size, I always got things larger than I needed, and wouldn't you take some of them for your best and I could keep some for my best and in that way———"

Two girls dividing pretty things seemed like a perfect setting for a lovely evening, but this calm could not last long. Even Aunt Bessie, who poked her head in and approved the girls' doings, could not hide her nervousness.

"Shall I hang these in your closet for you? Polly asked Cecy, picking up a lovely light blue ensemble that Cecy had taken among a lot of other pretty things.

"Yes, if you like—wait, I'll put them in," Cecy offered, remembering that the closet with the linen covered bag, that held the mysterious Indian shawl, was locked, and she would rather crowd the new things in the other closet than open it tonight.

But soon it would be gone, that shawl, and then there would be nothing more to hide.

"When," whispered Polly, "do you think we *can* see it? She wouldn't send it back without, would she?"

"I don't think so. Of course if we—got in a rush——"

They understood each other. If something happened and the shawl had to be rushed over to New York, how could they take time to see it? And here was their long quiet evening when they might have plenty of time, if only Aunt Bessie would consider it safe.

Long and quiet? That telephone jangled again. Aunt Bessie was not beside her extension now so Cecy hurried to answer it.

A man's voice asked if he could speak with Malika.

"Malika?" repeated Cecy, "there is no Malika here."

"She works here," the man insisted. "This is the home of Miss Benedict?"

"Yes, it is." Cecy was thinking fast. Of course this was one of those dangerous men looking for Malika.

"Then, she works there. She was there yesterday. She told me so herself."

"Who is this talking?" Cecy asked. As if it mattered.

"This is, I am her cousin in New York," came the reply.

"Oh, I see. I think Malika went to New York. I think she went this morning," murmured Cecy uncertainly.

"You are the young girl who lives with Miss Benedict?"

"Yes, I am. But Malika has not worked for us since—since we left the country. But I'm sure she has gone to New York. Perhaps she will see you—" What was she saying? And who was she talking to?

"Well, okay. She better come quick. If she has no job it is finished, then I guess she come quick, okay," and he hung up.

"Well, what do you think of that?" Cecy exclaimed, meeting the inquiring faces of Aunt Bessie and Polly. "We thought we would have some protection here and it's worse than ever. All they have to do is to telephone and what can we do but answer?"

"Now, don't get excited dear," cautioned Aunt Bessie. "It just might be that he *was* her cousin and she had been promising him some of her wages; they *all* have to pay relatives here after they come over, somehow. They always seem to owe debts in America before they get here."

But the girls knew that was just an excuse, and that the last voice over the phone was likely making sure he had the right place; Miss Benedict's apartment.

"Does Nora have to pay a lot of rent for this place, Aunt Bessie?" asked Polly, suddenly.

"Well, I thought she did, but she explained that in her last letter. A friend of hers had taken this apartment for the summer and later found she had to go abroad. So Nora took it, she said for very little, and it seemed just the thing for us."

"But you came here on my account, didn't you?" Polly asked next.

"Not entirely; partly. I could no longer stay out in that place safely, so I felt I should have to come where there was more protection. As I look at the whole thing now I can see I was just stubborn. I should have called in the right authorities and settled the whole thing. Girls, we've got a lot to do tomorrow, at least I have," she added wearily. "Don't you think we had better get quieted down and ready for bed?"

Ready for bed was simple enough, but quieting down did not seem so promising. Cecy could still feel her face burn from the excitement of trying to talk to that strange man, and Polly had not yet entirely recovered from her talk with Nora Grant.

As for Aunt Bessie— She was almost ready to get dressed then and there, so as to be out first thing in the morning to get to the bank about her business.

"There's a very fine man there, a Mr. Cooper," she told the girls as they attempted to talk things over. "He can advise me, I'm sure. And in these big banks they can call the highest authorities, if they need to."

"Then you are not going to give up the shawl unless he advises you to do so?" asked Polly, hopefully.

"He can tell me about the customs and look over my papers. I have them in a box at the bank," Aunt Bessie answered. "It still seems to me if I can prove I have bought and paid for the Old Rag and paid all the proper import charges on it, it would be better to get the authorities after that gang than to simply give up the shawl."

"But what about Malika?" asked Cecy. "You promised her you would save her father, you know."

"Yes, I know. And I hope to do that too," replied the mysterious Aunt Bessie.

"Did you get your letters written?" Polly asked Cecy. She had just carried into Cecy's room the little inlaid box from the desert. She was giving her that because she herself had another almost like it.

"I wrote a few. Oh, thanks, Polly, that's a lovely piece. Maybe you'd like to keep it for one of the girls out home, wouldn't you?"

"Oh, no, I'd like you to have this. See those curious Egyptian figures all made from small inlays." They fell to examining the delicate souvenir of the desert. Then Cecy asked:

"Have you any letters to mail? I'll put them out early, if you have."

"No, darling, not a let," said Polly softly. "You know something, Ceece? I was going to write to Bobbie Ellis."

"Well, why didn't you? Why not," Cecy assured her.

"I just couldn't think a thought, after or before Nora's phone. I've been wanting to tell you, Ceece. You know what really changed my ideas about all that—that pretense?"

"What?"

"Bobbie Ellis. He seemed to like me yet he would look at me so sort of curious. Then I knew he was looking through me, and I also knew I could not fool a nice boy like Bobbie."

"That's funny, Polly. When I met Bobbie, even before I met you, I had a feeling that he might help," said Cecy.

"You mean, show me how silly my attempt was?"

"Well, not just in that way," Cecy answered kindly. "But I've noticed before, that girls will trust boys and believe in them when they are timid or suspicious about girls. We had a girl in our class and everything all of a sudden seemed to go wrong with her. She shunned the girls and was getting frightfully nervous. When one of the quietest boys happened to walk home with her a few days, and——"

"I know. She got confidence and a new interest. Well, I've got all that too, now, Ceece. But I guess you're the one I ought to thank instead of Bobbie."

"I'll share the honors," smiled Cecy, giving Polly an awkward but affectionate squeeze.

CHAPTER XXII

THE CAPTURE

IT WAS arranged to have Polly go out with Aunt
Bessie to the bank next morning, and Cecy was to
stay in to be near the insistent telephone. Since
Irma would be there with Cecy that arrangement
seemed entirely satisfactory.

"And while I'm at the bank, Polly," Aunt Bessie
was planning, "Tom will drive you around to the
dress shop and you can select your dress."

"Oh, there's no hurry about that today," Polly
protested, rather wanting to stay in with Cecy.

"Well, I'd rather you did get a little dress, Polly
dear," Aunt Bessie said. She was just picking up
her handbag. "You see, we went in there the other
day, and I said one of you girls would come in
later."

"Oh, of course, Aunt Bessie. I'm all ready.
Come along, got everything?" Polly promptly
agreed.

Left to herself Cecy immediately phoned her
sister, Carol. She got her on the phone in the
nursery, and she tried without being too explicit, to

186

tell Carol about the change from Sylvia to Polly.

Carol, as usual most understanding, told her sister she had "done a good job" and after all, the lost vacation was turning out well worth while.

"Lost?" Cecy exclaimed at that. "With all my good hard earned money to show for it? No fooling, Sis, it is wonderful to be able to earn money. You know, I always envied you *your* luck. Well, I'll see you *very* soon—no, this is a real promise. I couldn't help breaking the others. I'll be down maybe tomorrow afternoon."

As Cecy turned away from the phone she remembered she had intended to ask Irma about watering the new fern, so she called to her. But there was no answer.

"Oh, she's gone down to the basement with the clothes for the laundress," Cecy recalled, going toward the potted fern in the little alcove to look it over.

Then the buzzer sounded. She stepped to the door and opened it.

"Good morning," said a young man pleasantly. "Mr. Scott sent me up to see if there's a short circuit here."

"*We* haven't had any trouble," Cecy quickly replied, realizing this was a stranger, although he did use Mr. Scott's name and although he was light, not dark like the others who had been threatening them.

"It was traced to this apartment," said the stranger, stepping in casually and swinging indifferently some sort of small tool. "The meter board is in a closet," he said, walking down the small hall toward the bedrooms.

Cecy was alarmed instantly. She called Irma but realized she was floors below in the laundry and might even stay there to do something for herself.

The man was moving about cautiously. "Is there a switch board in here, do you know?" he asked, his voice now taking on that corner of the mouth edge so typical of those who snarl at laws and locksmiths.

"No, I don't think there is," she replied evenly. Then she remembered that extra button Mr. Scott had shown her—the one that turned on the refrigerator. "Maybe this button—" she began, attempting to move toward it, and intending to touch it off —to touch anything off that might give an alarm.

"Stay where you are there!" came the sharp command, "and just save yourself a lot of trouble by telling me where *that* is. You know what I mean. The bag, suitcase, that's wrapped around with a cover. I've come for it and I'm going to get it this time, so you better hurry, because I'm in a hurry myself."

In spite of her panic Cecy knew she must be careful, a single false move and what could a girl do in the power of a man, likely armed? She just stood there against the wall frightened, helpless.

"Come on now, girlie," he snarled. "Which closet?"

He was in her own room and she had followed him there before he threatened her.

"Maybe this closet," he said, keeping one hand on the door jamb, which kept that hand almost within reach of her, and then he barely moved his head and shoulders inside.

Cecy watched him, scarcely breathing. He kept talking.

"You're all right, and you know what's good for you," he remarked sort of indifferently. It struck Cecy he was rather easy going for that sort of crime.

Next he said: "Yeah, I think I see something—" and then he stepped inside.

With a dash Cecy jammed the door on his hand, and as he cried out with pain he pulled his hand in and stepped in farther. The next moment Cecy had slammed the door shut and with one move she shot the brass bolt across.

Instantly the man began shouting and pounding, but Cecy turned and ran out into the hall, shouting and calling herself, although her voice seemed like a mere echo, she was so near collapse.

"What's this? What is all this?" It was Mr. Doyle.

"Oh, Mr. Doyle! Quick! I have a man locked in—no, don't go in alone," she begged. "Get help. He's safe—in the closet!"

After a little more explanation Mr. Doyle understood.

"You go over to that little corner house-phone," he directed her, "and call Mr. Scott. Tell him what's up and to bring his gun along with him."

Cecy followed his instructions as quickly as it was possible for her to move and to phone. "If only Irma doesn't come up the back way and just open that door!" she was sighing. She could hear the pounding even down the hall where she was now calling Mr. Scott. He came up on the elevator before she had hardly turned around, bringing two other housemen up with him. Cecy followed them in. She wanted to head off Irma coming up the backway.

Such a racket! Shouting and calling from the closet, and shouting and ordering from Mr. Doyle and Mr. Scott.

"Here," said Mr. Scott finally. "Call the police. One of you men——"

"I'll call," offered Cecy, glad to do something now that Irma was safely back in the kitchen and standing aside waiting to see what would happen next.

It was so much safer to have the police, Cecy knew. That man might just rush out when they opened the door and shoot any one in his path of escape.

The police seemed to get there at once. Cecy

was standing at the hall entrance now, Irma with her, to watch for Aunt Bessie and Polly, should they come along.

It was awful to see all those men in the apartment, yet how welcome they were.

The police were still talking to the man through the door, and now Cecy heard the bolt again shot back and a sort of struggle.

"They've got him," Irma whispered taking hold of Cecy's hand to give her confidence. "Now," Irma continued "everything will be all right. Hold on to me," she suggested, for Cecy was looking as she felt, pretty shaky.

"Oh, let's get back, here in this corner," Cecy whispered, for the men were coming; they were trouping out.

But the thief spied her as she tried to hide behind Irma.

"Little smartie, eh?" he sneered at her. "I oughta know'd better than to trust a girl your size. They're pretty smart——"

"Come along. That'll do y'a," said Dan Doyle. "Keep a civil tongue in your head and don't be insultin' the tenants."

So between two policemen, with Dan Doyle as advance guard, they led the blonde burglar away. Mr. Scott waited to speak to Cecy and Irma.

"That was smart work," he said to both of them.

"Oh, I was not here," explained Irma. "I had

just gone down to the laundry. It was Miss Duncan who captured him."

Then Cecy tried to tell Mr. Scott how it had happened. She did not, of course, say anything about the shawl and its threats. After all, Aunt Bessie had a right to her belongings and the old shawl was among them.

"But I was suspicious," Cecy told Mr. Scott, "the minute he stepped inside the door. He seemed in such a hurry."

"And regularly workmen don't usually rush around," said the superintendent, dryly. "But we know that fellow."

"You do?" Cecy exclaimed, in surprise.

"Yes. He's one of those scamps who hang around town and isn't particular what kind of job he attempts. I suppose someone else, probably from the city, heard there were rich folks in this apartment and got him to try his hands at doing a day-light burglary. You see, a very wealthy actress had this apartment formerly. It is sublet to Miss Benedict now."

When Mr. Scott finally left, he ordered one of the house boys to come in and move the upset furniture back into place.

"And you might as well stay here until Miss Benedict gets back," he told the boy. "Although, of course, the danger is all over now."

Cecy and Irma were glad to have Phil, the boy,

to talk to. He chatted away about other attempted burglaries, and how "some guys always think apartments are easy to rob," and how "swell" it was that Miss Duncan got him in that closet.

"A regular movie trick," he declared, pushing back a chair and rumpling up a rug that Irma would smooth out later. "I'll bet if they had a girl in a movie get a guy caught in a closet like that, and snap the bolt on him, they wouldn't believe it."

But Cecy wasn't gloating over her victory, by any means. She was wondering what would happen next. And if she and Aunt Bessie would have to go to the police station to make a charge against the man Phil was calling "a guy."

Cecy wouldn't like to have to do that.

CHAPTER XXIII

A LIVING STATUE

"To THINK that I missed it," wailed Polly.

"To think that I was lucky enough to miss it," added Aunt Bessie.

"Weren't you just scared to death?" Polly asked, wanting more and more of the horrible details.

"Yes, I was scared," Cecy admitted. "But when you get cornered like that you have to think fast."

"My dear child!" Aunt Bessie was murmuring. "To think that I should leave you here——"

"In broad daylight with Irma? Why not?" Cecy interrupted. "And don't you be afraid, Aunt Bessie, that my dad or my sister Carol will criticise us. They won't. Carol herself has been in plenty of exciting adventures and mine was tame compared to them. Polly, did you get your dress?" she asked, trying to change the subject.

But the subject wouldn't change. Polly had got the dress, she said, and it was sweet. "A little print." Why are dresses always "little?" But she wouldn't try it on to show it off. After lunch or even later, she promised, while Aunt Bessie continued to sniff around, as Cecy laughingly put it, looking for clues or something.

Soon Mr. Doyle was back, bringing the glad news that they would not have to make any charge at the police station.

"He's a knock-about fellow, they're always glad to pick up," Mr. Doyle explained. "He says some fellows who have been runnin' in and out from New York offered him a hundred dollars to get in here and get a bag, covered with linen, they said it was," Mr. Doyle said almost indifferently. "So of course, he said okay. And he tried to get it, well enough. But I doubt if I, myself, was here, could I have caught him as handy as that. It was a neat trick, Miss Duncan," he smiled at Cecy.

Everyone was too excited to enjoy lunch, but the peak was reached when Aunt Bessie promised the girls they could actually get the shawl out of its hiding place, and examine it to their hearts' content that very evening.

"You will have to see it tonight, if you're going to see it at all," she told them, "for I've arranged with the bank for them to get in touch with the customs at the Port of New York to have someone come here and examine it; I said I couldn't possibly take it over. They might declare it worth much more duty than I paid on it," she explained as the girls listened eagerly.

"But if they wanted more duty couldn't we pay

it?" Polly asked. She still hoped to get that prize for Nora.

"Oh, yes," Aunt Bessie replied wearily. "But I doubt if its value would be easily proved in this country. It's one thing to *have* an antique and quite another to find a market for it. I'm not one to go in for that sort of speculation," she said finally.

"But, at any rate, we will be able to look it over at last," Cecy put in, actually trying to console Polly. "And we'll have to be careful that no poisonous bugs or desert beetles are hidden in it. They might be, you know. They say such insects live for years without food or air."

But the subject failed to interest anyone. Polly was excited, but not about bugs or beetles, and Aunt Bessie was rejoicing that now, at last, they might have some peace, as the thieves would surely not come again soon.

"And even a little later will be too late," she said, "for in two days more Malika will know what we intend to do. If I can find out myself," she added, with a jolly little laugh. The afternoon seemed to drag, and the bright summer evening which settled down at last, seemed merely a lovely day prolonged —it just wouldn't get dark. They turned on the radio but it seemed there was static and no sign of storm.

"If we pull the shades down," murmured Polly.

"Yes, let's," said Cecy, anxious herself "for the show."

"Now wait," cautioned Aunt Bessie, "we mustn't take anything for granted. You say Irma went out, Cecy?"

"Yes. She's gone down to the post office."

"Then, please see that the rear door is locked. Irma can ring when she comes."

"I'll draw all the shades." Polly was rushing around.

"And let's draw the draperies too; that will give us a background," Cecy suggested.

"What is this going to be? Where do I sit? I'd like a ring-side seat," joked Aunt Bessie.

"That's it," chattered Polly, now really excited. "We *will* have a show. Where's the closet key, Cecy?"

"Whoa up there!" called Cecy. "If it's to be a show we have got to pitch our tent first. I always thought this place was fitted up for theatricals."

"Don't you remember what Mr. Scott said about the famous actress living here? Cecy, the key."

Cecy opened her regular closet door and pulled out a small shoe cabinet. From the bottom drawer she extracted a pink slipper.

"Not in that?" exclaimed Polly. "Why, that's the closet you snapped your burglar in and he might have kicked that over——"

"But see, dear. The key is in the toe and the slipper is all stuffed out with tissue. Here it is," and out came the precious key without even a bit of paper sticking to it.

"You open the door; it's your closet," said Polly.

"Afraid of those desert beasts? All right," and promptly Cecy unlocked the door.

After waiting so long the tenseness was understandable, for the old shawl in the linen-covered bag had gained with them a mythical significance. Cecy untied the little tapes on the linen cover and looked over at Aunt Bessie.

"Go right along," she told her. "I'm anxious to see the thing myself now. It's a long time since I put it in that bag."

The lights were on and the evening darkness had actually set in, so that there was no competition with shadows.

"Here," Polly suggested, "put it up on the bed. It might slip off the chair."

They giggled at her caution, thinking again: it might be alive!

The bag was open and Cecy went on unwrapping the tissue. The first layer of the old Kashmir was at last uncovered.

"Oh, it's white!" Cecy exclaimed, "with a lot of rose color embroidery."

All three of them now crowded around the old

piece of art, as Cecy very carefully unfolded parts
of it.

"The roses in the corners sort of stand out like
buds," Cecy remarked.

"Yes, and that's very unusual in a Kashmir,"
Aunt Bessie said. "Yes, that is a fine piece," she
was scrutinizing it with her strongest glasses," and
it's very old. Notice the white has softened into a
true ivory."

"Oh, I tell you!" exclaimed Polly. "Let me put
it on."

"Yes, you be the Indian Princess," suggested
Cecy. She knew how that would please the theat-
rical Polly.

"Yes. You both go out and I'll dress up. Then
I'll pose—in the living room?" she asked Cecy.

"Yes, of course, in the grandest setting as befits
a royal lady," Aunt Bessie answered first.

Cecy and Aunt Bessie waited in Aunt Bessie's
room while Polly dressed up. Every now and then
she would call out for instructions.

"They wore sandals, didn't they?" she asked
once. Then she decided she knew what would do
for sandals. Again she wanted to know should her
robe be long or short, and Cecy said the graceful
Indian princess, she believed, would show at least
one leg to the knee. "The one she was expected to
walk on," said Cecy. Which hobble idea brought

forth such a gale of merriment it almost spoiled the whole show.

Finally Polly said, "I'm almost ready and I'm going by your door. You are not to look until I get all posed. I'll let you know when."

They heard the lights snap on and off and finally Polly said in an absurdly affected voice:

"When!"

Cecy took Aunt Bessie's arm and they marched forward. The long velvet drapes of the dining room were parted just enough to afford their entrance. Directly inside were two chairs but they did not see them now.

They were looking at the little Indian princess.

"Oh!" gasped Aunt Bessie. "Be-au-tiful!"

Cecy was quite speechless.

Finally sinking into their waiting chairs they beheld what seemed to be a piece of statuary. A figure seated in the golden velvet chair draped with the fabulous shawl over her head and falling toward the floor, with one hand and bare arm just touching the folds to save it from that desecration. The head was inclined toward the round elaborate table on which stood a squat marble vase, very Egyptian. And one leg, the leg Cecy spoke of, was thrown over an arm of the chair and it showed its own flesh tints to the knee, as directed. The sandals were synthetic, being bits of pink satin ribbon (from two calendars) wound around the ankles of this en-

chanted princess. The only light in the room was
focused directly on the figure from a hidden table
bulb.

"Don't move," begged Cecy, "Aunt Bessie, isn't
she the real actress, though?"

"Real princess, I'd call her. If only we had a
camera for this light?"

"How'm I doin'?" giggled Polly, completely up-
setting the entire effect. "Shouldn't we have had an
audience?"

"With admission," concluded Cecy. "Honestly,
Polly, you should practice up. You would get there
in no time at all," Cecy declared.

CHAPTER XXIV

FULL MANY A GEM

EVEN all this spectacular beauty, together with its enfolding legends they seemed to feel was not enough to explain the priceless Indian shawl.

They looked at Polly, she changed her pose, and affected others equally exciting. Then she suggested that they watch her dance.

"You might get tripped up and tear the shawl," protested Cecy.

"Oh, no, I'll hold it up. I just want to show you. Ceece darling, may I have music?" she mimicked.

Cecy turned on the radio and very appropriately a solemn sort of arabesque rolled out from it.

Polly picked up her shawl and started. Not easy to fall into that rhythm at first, she finally slithered into it, swirled and twisted and reached for the stars, until some bursting seemed imminent. But she could dance, naturally; every note of the slow deep-toned music was emphasized by an original interpretation.

Then she attempted one of those high stepping poses, and threw one foot rather too high. It came down——

"Oh!" she screamed, and crumpled into the shawl on the floor.

"What is it?" cried Cecy, beside her instantly.

"My foot. Oh!" Polly had grasped a bare foot and was writhing in pain.

"Did something cut you?" Aunt Bessie demanded, trying to help Polly up to the chair.

"Or bite you?" asked Cecy, really serious now.

"No, it cut me, like a sharp point. Let me see," and instantly ignoring the injured foot Polly had grabbed up the shawl. "It was right here, this corner. I stepped on something."

"But let's fix your foot——"

"Oh, that's all right," Polly insisted. "I must see what it is. It felt like a piece of glass," and she was examining the shawl for the hidden weapon regardless of the injured foot.

"I always thought that shawl was loaded," Cecy grumbled.

Polly had gathered a small corner of the shawl in her hands and was fingering it carefully. She became so silently absorbed in the task that even Cecy's jokes did not distract her. Suddenly she looked up while holding on to that corner.

"Here!" she exclaimed. "I can feel it—right here."

"Let *me* see," Cecy begged.

"Wait, look. Here it is, right here. I've got it in my fingers——"

"What?" Cecy kept asking, as Aunt Bessie waited.

"Here, see here. Let's lay it on the table. I must keep it in my fingers, we might lose it," and Polly edged over to the table using her arm instead of her hands to push the book aside and make room for that corner of the shawl.

Cecy held the heavier part while they smoothed it out. Yes, there was something sharp in there, right in the heart of an embroidered rose. They were almost too excited to be as careful as they needed to be in handling the delicate old piece.

"Be careful not to break the threads," Aunt Bessie warned them. She was in the big chair at the other end of the handsomely carved table.

"We are just teasing them apart," Cecy explained. "That's what takes so long."

"I've got it," called out Polly. "Wait— Here! Oh! See!"

She was holding something up, something small and green and sparkling.

"A gem!" cried Cecy. "Look, Aunt Bessie, isn't it an—emerald?"

"An emerald!"

They were completely awestricken. For now Aunt Bessie held in the palm of her hand, sparkling in the light, a beautiful green gem. It was surely an emerald.

"Oh, it's yours, isn't it, Aunt Bessie?" exclaimed

Polly. "It was in the shawl and it's your shawl."
They both knew that Polly was thinking what a gift
that would be for Nora.

"Just wait a minute, girls," Aunt Bessie directed
them. She was turning the green stone over in her
hand, plainly mystified by its beauty.

"It is an emerald, isn't it, Aunt Bessie?" Cecy
asked, for they were all waiting anxiously.

"Oh, yes, it is. A very wonderful emerald————"

"And they are the most precious of all stones.
I know that," Cecy answered.

"More precious than diamonds?" Polly asked.

"Yes. The really fine emerald is more precious
than the diamond," Aunt Bessie stated. "You
know the emerald is even spoken of in the scriptures.
And you know the emerald was mined many thou-
sands of years before Christ," she went on, still
turning the stone over and over. It seemed to the
girls about as large as a dime, and it was easy to
understand how it had cut Polly's foot for the stone
itself would have cut if stepped upon.

"Tell us about emeralds, Aunt Bessie," urged
Cecy. "I've never seen a real one I suppose."

"Well, you remember hearing of Cleopatra's
Mines? There are plenty of interesting records of
emerald history," Aunt Bessie replied. "You'll
both have to read up on the subject now. But I can
tell you a few things even in a hurry. The emerald
was thought by the ancients to have curative powers,

which was naturally the virtue given it, because of its rarity and beauty. But this—this must be a really famous stone," she reflected, critically.

"Oh, just imagine! It was put in that shawl to hide it, wasn't it?" Polly asked eagerly.

"And, of course, it was the stone, not the shawl, that those men have been trying to get all the time; wasn't it?" Cecy asked. They could not restrain their questioning.

"Oh, most certainly," Aunt Bessie said. She still seemed too awestricken to know just what to say or to think about it all.

"Just let me hold it," begged Polly. She was still in her little silk slip, her arms and neck bare and the bits of ribbon clinging to her ankles.

"You might drop it in this deep-pile rug," objected Cecy.

"Oh, no. I'll hold it right over the table," Polly promised. Aunt Bessie then let the beautiful green stone slip into Polly's outstretched palm.

"Now, you are a real princess," she told her. "For certainly this stone could not have belonged to any one less."

It was hard to satisfy the girls' curiosity, but finally they came to the immediate question of what to do with the new-found treasure.

"You won't give it up, no matter what they say." That was Polly's insistent question.

"We can't tell; I don't know a thing about this,"

explained the perplexed lady. "I bought the shawl———"

"And all its embroidery and decorations; why not also the stone?" Cecy asked, reasonably.

"Let me see where this was hidden," Aunt Bessie demanded, and the girls had the spot ready to inspect immediately. Polly had put a book down on it so it couldn't slip away.

"I was surprised to see that these roses had been raised," commented Aunt Bessie. "Kashmir is always very flat."

"Do you think the shawl was made to hide the gem in it?" asked Cecy.

"No, that is hardly likely. But it might be that the gem thieves or whoever they were who had this gem, were looking for a piece of embroidery to hide it in and somehow found this, and it answered perfectly."

"Of course we don't know the story," Cecy added. "It might be that Malika's father just agreed to keep the shawl, sort of in storage, and by accident it got in with the goods he had for sale."

"That's very likely a good guess. But see, here's a tiny scrap of very fine paper. The stone must have worked its way out of it."

A new surprise. And yes, and there were almost invisible marks on the tiny piece of old India paper.

Naturally they examined the scrap, smoothing it out and putting a flash light over it, but while marks could be seen, it was not possible to identify them. They decided they might be a number which would some time give the clue to the emerald's place in the world of precious stones.

"It may be a museum piece; many gems have been stolen from museums. Well, now are we going to sit up all night to watch it?" Aunt Bessie had taken the prize from Polly, and while instinctively they were glancing apprehensively at the windows, the fear of that sort of intrusion had gone with the capture of Cecy's burglar. There seemed to be no danger now of anyone else trying to get in.

"Perhaps there's a large reward out for it," Polly ventured, when finally she was ready to put a common every day robe over her princess slip, and stick her toes into her blue mules.

"I'm sure there must be," Aunt Polly agreed to that speculation. "And the easiest way for me to find out will be through the custom's man who will be out from New York tomorrow."

"Will it be in the papers?" Polly asked.

"Not if I can keep it out," said Aunt Bessie. "After all, if this proves to be—mine, and I bought the shawl for Nora——"

"Let Nora get all the publicity," cried Polly. And her gratitude to the actress, Nora Grant, did not seem out of place just then.

CHAPTER XXV

OF PUREST RAY SERENE

"THERE's nothing like a couple of cops to liven things up." And certainly the man who said that liked things lively. It was the watchman, Dan Doyle.

Now, early in the morning after the exciting night before, Aunt Bessie with Cecy and Polly were having a few moments rest from answering the telephone. No sooner had Aunt Bessie told Mr. Cooper of the local bank that "there had been exciting new developments in the matter she had consulted him about the day before" than the wires began to buzz.

But now here was Mr. Doyle and he was giving a sort of report about "the feller they picked up yesterday."

"I knew him, of course," Mr. Doyle said a little boastfully, "and I suspected he had been hired by someone smarter than he thought he was, and wasn't. Well, I suppose he had it all arranged to meet these fellers when they got off the train this morning. But he wasn't there; the cops was."

"You mean there were men from New York

waiting for that man Cecy caught?" Polly asked.
She found Mr. Doyle's speech hard to understand.

"Right there at the station," he answered her.
"And quick as they stepped off the train and gave
one good look around our officers stepped up to
them and it was all over."

"What did they do?" Aunt Bessie asked. Like
Polly she too found it hard to follow Dan Doyle.

"Took them over to our police station here," he
told her. "There they had a talk with Flicker;
that's what they call the guy you caught here," he
turned to Cecy to tell her, "and, of course, Flicker
went for them. He, it seems had no idea of getting
into all that trouble."

"Will we have to do anything about that?   I
mean with the police?" Aunt Bessie asked him.

"Not a thing.   They took him to New York with
the other fellers a while ago, and it's just as well to
have Flicker some place else than hanging around
that station," said Mr. Doyle.   Of course he knew
nothing at all about the shawl and even less than
nothing about the emerald.   All *he* needed to know
was that some "feller" tried to burgularize the
apartment where Dan Doyle was watchman; that
was enough for Dan.

When he left them and a few more phone calls
were attended to, Cecy ventured to ask Aunt Bessie
what she would do about Malika.   She was to phone
Aunt Bessie the next morning and then Aunt Bessie

was to give her positive assurance about her father's release from that prison, away off in the shadow of the pyramids.

"At first that seemed like something I couldn't arrange in so short a time," Aunt Bessie answered Cecy. "But Mr. Cooper tells me the customs men at New York are in direct touch with all points in the world. And you know a cable now to Egypt is not much more difficult to handle than our long distance telephones. The systems of communication have been so perfected lately we scarcely have to wait at all.

"I told Mr. Cooper I was anxious to have this old man secure his liberty, if they find he was only a tool in that international ring, as I believe he was. Mr. Cooper said the officials at the Port of New York would be able to get in touch with the officials at Cairo very promptly. So I can tell Malika that, and she can go to the office and get further assurance if she wants to, but as Peter says, 'she's afraid of cops' so I guess she'll take my word for it," smiled Aunt Bessie.

Polly had beckoned Cecy into her room, to whisper a few very private questions.

"But if Aunt Bessie is going out to the country house again, as she says she is, and this place is to be given up the first of the month, we'll all scatter, won't we?" she asked plaintively.

"But we have to scatter anyhow in about a week,"

Cecy reminded her. "Aren't you just crazy to get back to your folks in Melody Lane?"

"Oh, of course I am. You have no idea what it means——" Polly stopped and seemed to be pondering. There was nothing left now of the girl who had played Sylvia except a few nice clothes, some bits of jewelry and a lot of memories, some bitter, some sweet. But no one now would dare to use that odious term snob, in referring to Polly.

"And I'm going back to my family like the prodigal," added Cecy. "I hope they'll take me in. Then, Polly, you know Carol and I and even Dad still love Melody Lane so 'we'll be seein' you.' " She added the common phrase to relieve the possible sentimental strain she thought she saw creeping into Polly's hazel eyes.

"Girls, there's the buzzer," came a call from Aunt Bessie, and there was no more time for confidences.

It was Mr. Cooper and a customs official. Polly and Cecy felt pretty important after that, helping Aunt Bessie get the shawl out to have it inspected, and then getting out her jewel case. Aunt Bessie took the case and carefully untied the small chamois bag in which the emerald was secured.

"Here it is." That was all she said. Then the custom's official took out his magnifying glass and began his preliminary inspection.

Cecy and Polly were seated on the little divan in

the corner and every few seconds one or the other would squeeze each others hand. They were so anxious to know. Was it a real emerald? Could it be an imitation?

The inspector took his own glasses off, laid down his magnifying glass and after an endless time looked up with tantalizing deliberation before he spoke. Finally he said to Mr. Cooper:

"That's it, Clifford; that's the long lost Muzo Emerald, and it belongs to one of the potentates of India."

No one spoke for a few seconds. While not fully understanding the importance of his announcement, even Polly knew that it *was* important.

"Are you sure?" asked Mr. Cooper, whom the man had called Clifford.

"Positive. See how it takes the light." He put his left hand half way over the stone as he held it in his right hand. "Now it is a bluish green, notice?"

"Yes," replied Mr. Cooper, "but I don't think it really shows much fire?"

"That's the sign of the true emerald. It has invisible lines, many of them that add to that deep color. In the dichroscope it would give a true blue green and even a yellow green image. It's that strangely deep color, not its brilliance, that gives the stone its value," he said, very scientifically.

Then Aunt Bessie gave the men the little bit of tissue paper, and, of course, it did not take the expert long to decide that this was a tangible proof of the authenticity.

The girls were mystified. They both just liked the gorgeous stone and were thrilled with the prospects of its great value. All this scientific rating rather went over their heads.

"There's a reward of twenty-five thousand dollars standing right here with an American insurance company for that stone," went on the man Mr. Cooper called Theodore. His name, it seemed, was Theodore Young and he and Mr. Cooper were well acquainted. "Those Indian princes pay fabulous sums for their gems, and they even maintain private vaults here in America to guard them. When some wealthy American lets it be known that he has some unique stone for sale, the agents of these potentates pick it right up. Miss Benedict," he turned to Aunt Bessie, "I'll take all the data you can give me now. It will save you trouble and I can get right on the case."

In telling her long story, of how she had acquired the shawl and only just now discovered the emerald, both Cecy and Polly felt they had taken part in a great drama, even if Polly did have to have her foot pricked to allow the gem-fairy a chance to make itself known.

It took more than two hours to satisfy Mr. Young that he had obtained all the particulars. When finally he took the stone, carefully folded the bit of paper, and putting it with the emerald snapped it shut tight in a very small case he was carrying in the inside upper pocket of his coat, everyone seemed rather relieved that the ordeal was over.

"But the shawl?" Polly sort of whispered.

"Better keep that," Mr. Thompson said. "There may be a call for it as part of the evidence against the smugglers and thieves in their plot. It's pretty, isn't it?" he said in a man's indifferent way. As if it were only just pretty!

"Now," said Aunt Bessie with a deep sigh, "if only I can get in touch with Nora, I want to know if *she* wants that stone or——"

"She'll want *you* to have the money, Aunt Bessie. I'm sure she will," Polly stated, very emphatically, "Of course, Nora is rich, but after all she's not that rich," she finished, rather a new tune for Polly to be singing, who possibly had been thinking about giving things like the Indian shawl to her idol. But twenty-five thousand dollars!

"We'll all be rich," sighed Aunt Bessie finally, and in spite of their protests she was planning to have these two girls share at least a small part of that insurance reward.

But both Cecy and Polly smothered her compliments with what seemed to be a real lively bit of hugging. And who could blame them for that?

THE END